A PLACE
OF TIMELESS
HARMONY

CURT ERIKSEN

Texas Review Press
Huntsville, Texas

FIRST EDITION
Requests for permission to acknowledge material from this work should be sent to:
     Permissions
     Texas Review Press
     English Department
     Sam Houston State University
     Huntsville, TX 77341-2146

Cover design: Veronica Sosa Design—www.veronicasosa.com
Cover photo: Curt Eriksen—www.curteriksen.com

Library of Congress Cataloging-in-Publication Data

Names: Eriksen, Curt, author.
Title: A place of timeless harmony / Curt Eriksen.
Description: First edition. | Huntsville, Texas : Texas Review Press, [2017]
   Identifiers: LCCN 2017023927 (print) | LCCN 2017030556 (ebook)
| ISBN
   9781680031461 (ebook) | ISBN 9781680031454 (pbk. : alk. paper)
Subjects: LCSH: Tanzania--Fiction. | Man-woman relationships--Fiction.
Classification: LCC PS3605.R52 (ebook) | LCC PS3605.R52 P58 2017
(print) |
   DDC 813/.6--dc23
LC record available at https://lccn.loc.gov/2017023927

For M.J.
Jessica, Eloy and Ian

Dread, it would seem, the ensnaring reality, best set in dreams, enhances—perhaps even makes possible—beauty.

Theodore Weiss
The Man from Porlock

Existence was governed by fantasy and superstition.

Richard Hall
Empires of the Monsoon

A PLACE
OF TIMELESS
HARMONY

I

After Gibb's Farm it was never going to be the same. But Sofie didn't know that when she exclaimed, "What is this? Paradise?"

She said this after they'd pulled up in front of the gate of the coffee plantation grounds, set high on the outer lip of the Ngorongoro Crater, some 2,000 meters above the level of the sea where—less than a week ago, and over five hundred kilometers away, while lying on the sands of Pemba, alone—Zuri had approached her and stood, with his cryptic shadow cast across her flat and hollowed belly, asking her whether or not she spoke any Swahili.

Bouncing along the roughly graded lane bordered by the greedy evergreens—the yellowwood and bushwillow and Spanish tamarind, the honeysuckle and liana and other creepers that were all coated with the fine red dust that the four-wheel-drives churned up as they came and went, delivering their packages of wide-eyed tourists to the entrance of Gibb's Farm—Sofie had chosen not to mention the pain again. None of it. Ever.

But she had wondered aloud whether or not it was going to be as marvelous as Richard had promised it would be. All she could see through the dust-glazed window before they reached the ornate iron gate that marked the entrance to Gibb's Farm were the barefoot coffee pickers, ambling along the edge of the tamped clay road, with their heads hanging and their empty buckets swinging from their loose black fingers.

Mwenge—always eager to ingratiate himself by providing his charges with relevant tidbits of information—had explained that these men and women were required to purchase the buckets themselves, and this fact seemed to Sofie like another petty injustice, and another slap in the face. One more cruel and bitter degradation, suffered under the grinding boot heel of free enterprise.

But Richard had tilted his head to one side, thoughtfully nodding his chin. As if he both understood and agreed with the idea that these day laborers couldn't possibly be trusted to take care of the buckets and bring them back if they didn't own them.

"A small, but essential investment?" he said, offering the observation as if it were a question. "A stake in the game. Right? An incentive. And another example, I suppose, of the way micro-financing can work."

Sofie knew him well enough to know that this comment was meant to be taken by Mwenge—who replied by saying, "Yes, that is so"—as sincerely intended, and only mildly patronizing. Leaving the implied sarcasm for her alone to chew on.

Just as her efforts, during the past six months, to learn enough of the language these people spoke to at least thank them for their many courtesies—*asante, asante sana*—were regarded by Richard as another of her many caprices. Which he would always be happy to indulge.

But there was no indulging what had happened deep inside of her recently. It wasn't only the "little correction," the "sorting out of the problem," as one staffer at the clinic had put it, the "procedure" that Sofie had so reluctantly agreed to in the end, in response to Richard's unrelenting insistence that the timing "just isn't right."

There was also that unaccountable transformation that Sofie had begun to feel before she became so sick last June that she needed a dose of antibiotics, hence the failure of the birth control

2

pills. A transformation occasioned by a weary seepage of faith in any real future with Richard, and the prospect of the two of them ever becoming us. A change she only became aware of a couple of months later, after that brief burst of renewed optimism preceeding the abortion had been callously extinguished along with the life inside her. A change that only became absolutely clear to Sofie once she and Richard had arrived in Tanzania, when she lowered her sunglasses enough to see over them and made out Zuri standing above her on the beach, with his slender silhouette dark and pole-like against the vast East African sky.

For a moment though, none of that seemed to matter. For a moment it was as if everything that had happened recently might still be erased, or reversed. Or as if none of what had happened had really happened at all, and therefore need not be remembered, and agonized over. For a moment it was as if everything could be forgotten. Even if nothing could be forgiven.

When the Land Rover came to a stop in front of the gate Richard pushed open the door and stepped down and, gentlemanly as always, offered a hand to help Sofie out. Two elegant and dignified hosts wearing *shukas* approached them. One of these thin dark men draped in the red checked cloth typical of the Maasai carried a tray of moistened hand towels, while the other presented the Americans with a pair of stemmed glasses filled with freshly squeezed passion-fruit juice.

"What is this place?" said Sofie, accepting the offer to refill her glass as soon as she had swallowed the sweet liquid. Wiping the sweat and dust off the back of her neck she looked around at foliage so dense and greenly inscrutable, so lush and insanely verdant, that she couldn't even be sure of what she was seeing. "Paradise?"

Richard was, in some ways at least, like the satellites he leased, untethered and often floating in space. And sometimes cold and steely too. All over the place, much of the time. Restless, and not as often around as Sofie would have liked. And certainly not as much hers—all hers, and *only* hers—as she claimed she wanted him to be.

His company—Ardcom—was co-owned by two other equal partners, Andersen and Rivas (Richard's surname was Delmore). Ardcom's mission, as stated on its website, was "to provide essential tracking and communications services" via hardware that his international clients could either not afford to purchase outright, or preferred not to purchase outright, but could not possibly function without, and therefore had to lease.

When asked, Richard would always say simply, "I work in telecommunications." If gently pressed, when relaxed and at ease, once the single malts—never, so long as there was any choice, aged less than sixteen years—had softened the teeth of his anxieties, he might admit that he was the master of many eyes in the sky. Any one of which was capable of telling you where you were, and what you were wearing, and who you were with, at any time, on any day of any week, during the past two decades.

Sofie's mother, when she met him, was not only curious, but genuinely intrigued. Richard was precisely the sort of man she herself was looking for—matured just enough by the onerous demands of a still-growing family somewhere in the background, with plenty of hair on his head touched by streaks of debonair graying, well-groomed and cleverly dressed, both fit and smart, and earning by now more money than he could hope to spend in a lifetime—but she had no intention of competing with her daughter for his favors. She would happily flirt and tease Richard, when alone with him, and insinuate when alone with Sofie that this might not be such a very good idea after all, that the seventeen years and eight months between them and the fact that Richard was still married was a little much. But otherwise she had promised herself that she wouldn't interfere. Isabella swore to herself, and pledged that she wouldn't. Instead she said only, once Richard had expounded a bit

4

on his line of work, that she'd be very interested in meeting some of his "spy friends."

Richard preferred not to think of Bella—as she insisted he call her—at all. He knew he was right not to trust her, but he wasn't sure why he didn't trust her. When she stared at him across the table at Testa's, on that first night, with eyes that seemed simultaneously sad yet sparkling, offering him a look that let him know exactly what she was thinking, he had to turn away, something he wasn't used to doing, averting his eyes from a challenge. His motto had always been to look straight and hard at anything that came at him.

But Bella seemed to peer inside of him, shining an unwelcome light in dark corners that Richard himself had chosen not to inspect, or even admit were there. Turning away from her proud and still handsome mother, he couldn't rest his gaze and linger on Sofie either, something he had so often enjoyed doing, a passive yet observant activity that had already brought him more pleasure than he felt that he deserved. Because Sofie was not only radiant and unsuspecting, and certain that this first meeting was going better than she had hoped: she was trusting of Richard in a way that sometimes made Richard feel like a predator.

"My friends aren't spies," he said, without bothering to add that they weren't really his friends either, not at all. Dabbing his lips with the corner of his napkin he explained, "My business partners may be cunning, but they're not brave. They lead eventful, but unimaginative, and in some ways almost spiteful, lives. They close deals and celebrate by ostentatiously inviting strangers to thousand dollar bottles of champagne. They fly out to Aspen, ski half a day, and play squash that same evening at the Commodore, in St. Paul. They use the Learjet, but each has his own man and they bicker over who gets to pilot the jet. They let someone else chauffer them about town, while they thumb through The Wall Street Journal and glance at the Tourneaus and Vacherons on their wrists when the traffic slows. They express their annoyance and benevolent disdain with people they regard as their underlings by subtle shifts of their eyelids. Have you ever noticed something like that, Bella? In others, I mean?"

"Even though they don't want to admit it," he continued, "my partners are nothing but technicians. Financial technicians. Very good at numbers, and making brutal, and often heartless, decisions. Crafty and Machiavellian, certainly, but in other ways barely literate. We went to college together, and that's about all we have in common. That, and the fact that we just happened to come up with the same idea, at the same time."

Richard studied the tumbler he held in his hand as if it might tell him why he had let all of this out now. But he didn't rue the fact that it was happening, that he was being so much more forthright on this first evening with Sofie's mother than he had intended to be.

Ready at last to meet Bella's arch dismay, if that's what it was, he lifted his eyes and said to her, "So it was easy, almost as if it were meant to be, when we found ourselves bending an elbow at the same watering hole, at the same boring Chicago convention, each of us working at jobs we weren't entirely satisfied with, not so very long after completing our MBAs and going our separate ways and never expecting to see each other again. By the end of that night we had agreed that the idea was solid, and we figured out how we would go about collecting the venture capital. We shook on it and left the hotel, where we'd bribed the barman to stay up with us and ply us with drink throughout the night. He was the one who recommended the diner where we went to get something to eat. Greasy eggs and bacon, proletariat fare, that's what we were after. It was as close as I've ever been to those men, walking down the same dirty sidewalk on a cold November morning, sleepless and convinced like they were that we would soon be dining on caviar and truffles. And"—he drained the last of the whisky in his tumbler and allowed a smug, if theatrical, lifting of his own eyebrow—"it's worked out rather nicely since. That's all."

After a bath together in the polished stone tub that was as big as the Delmore's jacuzzi, they made love on the bed without bothering to dry off. It was the first time since the abortion that Sofie had welcomed Richard, and positively wanted him inside of her again. But while he was pleasuring her, before mounting her, it was Zuri she saw when she closed her eyes.

Together they lay in the cool of the room that was tempered by the fire crackling in the grate. Sofie's head rested on Richard's chest and she could hear his heart slowing down. She had never known her father and never much wanted to know him, at least not until that budding life that would have been his too—in a way—was scraped and sucked out of her womb.

Now there wasn't anything she could say to Richard, so she didn't speak. She let him trace his fingers along her shoulder blade and down her back and over the curve of her hip, again and again, stroking her the way he liked to do. Then she got up and opened the closet and stood in the light that came on as soon as she pulled on the handle of the closet door. She could feel Richard looking at her, appraising and appreciating her, but also wondering. Sofie slipped her arms through the sleeves of one of the clean white terrycloth bathrobes and, without giving Richard a backward glance, padded into the bathroom.

The large granite tub was set in a corner of the spacious bathroom, and the walls surrounding it and the stone sink were windowed to the ceiling. A pair of French doors opened onto the wooden balcony, where there was an outdoor shower and a waist-high latticework bamboo railing. The balcony was raised high above the walkway below, and the only thing Sofie could see through all that glass was that same impenetrable green, in every direction, where so much invisible life must be determinedly carrying on.

They sat at a small table in the intimate dining room with its tasteful selection of African artifacts decorating the walls, near a window overlooking the hills planted with row after row of coffee shrubs. Dusk was rapidly ceding to night, as it always does near the equator, and the rows of coffee shrubs seemed to melt into the spreading darkness. But there was none of that uneasy foreboding that Richard had felt when they were eating dinner by lantern light in the dining tent in Tarangire.

This was the sort of thing he was more accustomed to: the fine food and excellent wine, the red candle burning in the middle of the cozy table, the efficient and courteous service. Whereas eating and sleeping with nothing but a sheet of canvas separating them from the marauding wildlife drawn to the campsite by the scent of water had not only been exhilarating: it had reminded him, constantly, of how close death was.

And how it always crept up on you. Regardless of whether it struck quick, or slow.

But they had made love again, and that was something to celebrate. Sofie had groaned and shuddered and Richard had felt, if only for a moment, that they had a whole life to live yet in which they might be melded together at last. Sitting across the table from her, watching her lovely mouth, seeing the glitter in her ears of the pair of tanzanite stones he'd bought for her at the arts and craft shop on the way there, with the hope precisely of improving her mood and encouraging her forgiveness, made him feel so fortunate that he was overwhelmed with joy and gratitude. And able to forget, if only momentarily.

Of course everything would work out! And she might still bear his child. Assuming he were able to overcome this.

After dinner they walked along the paths lit by judiciously placed lanterns. The whiffs of kerosene smoke among the cool scents

8

of the luxuriant foliage in the chill mountain air were reassuring. Richard and Sofie walked with their arms around each other, with no objective other than that of being together like this, in this place, now.

When they got into bed they warmed themselves with the heat of the other's skin. Even though they would be getting up before daylight they were in no hurry at all. Sofie was behaving now as if none of it had ever happened. Or at least as if none of it had mattered enough to destroy any of all that they had managed to build together during the past three years. She seemed to Richard to open herself to him again. It was as if the shutters had been raised, and the moonlight were pouring in. They rose together towards a climax they might have shared, and before drifting off Sofie whispered something near Richard's ear that he didn't quite catch. It might have been some sort of an apology. But he was too pleased and sleepy to bother asking her to repeat it.

When the knock on the door came it was still night. Out of the darkness a velvety voice called, "Jambo jambo."

Sofie flicked on the bedside light and found the robe she'd discarded on the floor. The polished wood planks were icy beneath her feet. "What is it?" murmured Richard, more asleep still than awake yet.

Sofie cinched the robe around her waist and opened the door saying "Karibu" the way she'd heard the natives say it, drawing the 'u' out so that the invitation to come in sounded like a lilting line from a melodious song.

"Habari za asubuhi?" said the man, inclining his torso almost imperceptibly as he entered.

"Nzuri sana," said Sofie, stepping aside as he carried the tray with the pot of tea and the small sugar bowl and the little cream pitcher in the shape of a rooster into the sitting area of the large room. He set the tray on the table and she said, "Asante sana."

"Karibu sana," said the man, bowing again, just as imperceptibly, as he backed out of the room. With a little click he pulled the door shut behind him.

Sofie stood for a moment listening to the light tread of the man's footsteps as he walked down the stone path that led away from their room. It was still too dark, too early yet, for the rioting of the rousing birds. Instead there were only the shy gossiping shrieks of the bush babies. And beyond that the more unpredictable, the unidentifiable, and sometimes strangled cries of the other night creatures.

Sofie poured the steaming tea into two cups. She sugared and creamed Richard's tea and carried both cups on saucers to the bed, where she sat on the edge of the mattress and told him it was time to get up.

→ →⟩ →⟩ →⟩

Mwenge was waiting for them with the Land Rover in the circular drive. After greeting each other with the standard formalities—*Jambo?* and *Habari gani?*—he said to Sofie, "Umeamkaje?"

"Nimeamka vizuri," said Sofie. Followed by something else in Swahili that sounded like a question.

"Short night," replied Mwenge, turning the key in the ignition. "Karatu is my home. Whenever I come here I must visit my people. We drink, and play poker. And one beer is never enough. Pombe moja kamwe haitoshi."

Mwenge chuckled, as he shifted into gear and lifted his eyes to glance at Sofie in the rearview mirror. She smiled, but did not reply to what must have been some sort of joke, as they pulled away from the entrance to Gibb's Farm.

Richard appreciated the fact that Mwenge was polite enough

to respect his ignorance of the language, and usually reverted to English, at least in his presence. At any rate he couldn't be sure how much more Sofie would have been able to say to the guide in Swahili. Richard did not know and could not judge the extent of her knowledge of the language. Though everyone she spoke to complimented her on her "excellent pronunciation."

Coming down the hill from Gibb's Farm they saw the coffee pickers on their way to work. The overhanging trees lining the road formed a tunnel-like grove. They passed gaggles of school children walking along the verge in truly ragged uniforms that must have been patched up until there was practically nothing left to stitch, as these uniforms were handed down through generation after generation. Both the girls and the boys shaved their heads and the only way to tell the difference between them was by the skirt or pants they were wearing, either maroon or blue. The Land Rover sped along the unpaved road, kicking up a streaming cloud of red dust, as it overtook the men riding two-wheeled carts pulled by a pair of lumbering oxen.

Then they were on the asphalt highway, hurling past the clusters of motorcycle taxis waiting for riders at every intersection. Soon the road began to rise again. There was no sun, the clouds were low, and Richard could see nothing of the extinct volcanic rim that he knew was up there, high above them, somewhere. Finally they turned off the highway and began climbing the shoulder of the crater.

It was cold inside the unheated Land Rover, and Richard took Sofie's hand. She looked at him, almost regretfully, and her lips parted slightly, as if she might have wanted to say something to him. But she didn't. So he had no idea what she might be thinking.

They continued racing up the narrow and winding road slung over with low leafy branches, through patches of dense fog, the taillights of the next vehicle in front of them blinking briefly before disappearing around another curve. Mwenge had mentioned the superiority of the Land Rovers over the Land Cruisers and he drove with the determination to prove this superiority at every opportunity. But Sofie didn't seem to mind.

At the gate to the Ngorongoro Crater they had to wait while Mwenge stood in line with all the other guides and filled out the necessary papers and paid the park fees. He used to be a ranger inside the crater and he'd told them that when the Maasai were driven out of the crater in 1975 the poachers moved in, halving the elephant population and almost wiping out the rhinos within a decade. That was when the poachers started using the weapons that were made available by the fallout from the Ogaden War, between Somalia and Ethiopia.

"When the Somalis invaded Ethiopia the Russians didn't like it. So they changed sides. The Americans also changed sides, giving their guns to Somalia. So both sides had plenty of guns. After that," he said, "everyone carried assault rifles. Including the rangers."

The tour of the crater—technically a caldera—was uneventful. They saw plenty of wildebeest and zebra grazing side by side, and lots of Thomson's gazelles, and blubbery slumbering hippos nose-deep in the crowded hippo pond. There were wart hogs unexpectedly dashing here and there, as if on urgent missions, with their short antenna-like tails sticking straight up in the air. And they came across a pack of sated hyenas lying on their sides in the tall dry grasses, only a few meters from the dirt track, their bellies so full from a night of feasting that they could barely bother to open their eyes to see who it was that had stopped to stare at them.

There was a lone bull elephant in the gray distance, surprisingly solitary, its trunk hanging between a pair of magnificent tusks, a little depressing to see, though stately, on that cold overcast morning. And small herds of other bachelors banded together, the older Cape buffaloes that had been driven out by the younger and stronger bulls.

Mwenge explained that these males sought each other out and stayed together for mutual protection against the lions that were so hard to discover during the day. Richard thought about this and said, "In other words, once these bulls aren't fit enough to dominate, it's all over? They're exiled? And can only look forward to eating grass, until they themselves are eaten?"

"Or die a natural death," suggested Mwenge.

There were supposed to be twenty-six black rhinos left in the crater, and Sofie saw one of them, through the binoculars, sitting on the ground with its prehistoric legs folded beneath its armored chest, not far from the shores of the stinking soda lake, its heavy head raised just high enough to produce a silhouette of horn and one immobile leaf-shaped ear. Like some great bronze sculpture, erected upon extinction.

But no lions. And no kill.

Sofie didn't hunger for violence, but she did want to see some action. Something more, anyway, than the scuttling wart hogs.

When the Land Rover eased its way through the masses of seemingly indifferent zebra and wildebeest that stood in the road, parting these herds the way the prow of an icebreaker cuts a path through the frozen sea, she felt like jumping out and flailing her arms. Anything to get more of a reaction out of these alert, yet tranquil, ungulates than that of merely staring back at her.

Not that she wasn't satisfied—or at least that's what she told herself—with seeing all these animals in their natural habitat. It was eerily beautiful inside the crater, especially once the clouds lifted enough to make visible the curved rim of its forested lip, circling them no matter which way they turned. And the way that eternal wind blew across the golden-yellow plain, whispering through the dry grasses, moved her to speculate upon the dignity of a world no human had ever laid eyes on.

But even though Mwenge assured them that these animals were as wild—if not as skittish—as any animals they would ever come upon, the outing felt too much like a drive through Lion Country Safari in Loxahatchee, a mere forty-five minute drive from Bella's new Palm Beach condo. Except that there weren't any lions here. Or at least none that Sofie could see.

Richard had resolved to speak to Sofie, and tell her about the prognosis, but he kept waiting for the right moment. He knew, of course, that no such thing as the right moment existed. The opportunity had to be created, the moment had to be made. It wasn't going to present itself of its own accord.

All day he had thought about this, while they were driving around in the Land Rover, looking for more animals to tick off the list of those they had come here hoping to see. Richard knew that Sofie wanted to see the big cats, and so did he. Mwenge was surprised that they hadn't come across any lions. The grass wasn't as high as it grew in the rainy season, but there were 260 square kilometers in which the lions might be resting. Mwenge had explained that there were four prides in the crater, and none of them ever ventured into the others' territories. "That's what the males are for," he said, "to make sure everyone respects the rules." The only explanation that made any sense to Mwenge was that all four prides had been both active and successful during the night and that the lions—like the spotted hyenas they had seen—were sleeping it off somewhere, just out of sight.

Richard thought of how they could have been lying like the hyenas in the grass that was practically the same color as the lions' fur. All it would have taken to have seen one of the lions was the lifting of a head, or the swishing of a tail.

But that hadn't happened. And as they headed back to Gibb's Farm—climbing the one-way road that had recently been paved, the only way out of the crater—Sofie's silent disappointment weighed upon Richard and he decided that telling her about the results of the tests tonight would not be a good idea.

Because there had always been this too in their relationship: his fear not so much of losing Sofie, as of letting go of her.

Richard knew that Sofie was the one who had made it happen, she was the one who had chosen him, even though she didn't see it that way. And since she had chosen him, he reasoned, she could just as easily *not* choose him anymore. It was as simple as that.

So Richard held on to Sofie. Like a boy flying a kite.

Of course the way Sofie saw it, Richard could have had anyone he wanted. He was eminently successful, with lots of interesting connections, and still handsome, perhaps even more handsome than ever now that he was over fifty. And although the external accoutrements of his life resembled those of his business partners, there was that something else in him that had so immediately attracted Sofie's attention. According to her it was a teenager's sullen rebellious streak, buried deep beneath Richard's charming speech and manners. Not many people saw this in him, it was barely discernible, she said, in the occasional melancholy note in his voice, something he usually managed to mask and hide in public, an instinctively repressed yearning that made the charming speech and manners all the more alluring and irresistible. Or that, anyway, was how Sofie had always described her attraction to him.

Early in the relationship, when Richard had told her that he didn't think he'd be able to leave Andrea until the twins had finished high school, Sofie had replied by saying, "Then the best thing you could do, the right thing to do, would be to let me go."

That night they separated with the certainty that it was over and Richard went home determined to do precisely that, to forget about Sofie. For a week there was no communication between them whatsoever. But Richard couldn't shake the sense of grieving. How was it, he wondered, that he had come to depend upon this woman—upon the fact of her existence in his life—so much, so soon? His depression was noted at home, and he lied and attributed this to business concerns. "But it's not bad enough," he had assured his wife, "that you need to worry about it."

When Richard couldn't resist the temptation any longer he called Sofie, just to see how she was getting along. For a while they simply listened to the other breathing on the far end of the line. Then Sofie asked him if he wanted to come over. While they were making love Richard felt the reckless passion and desire to fill her with his seed, and make her pregnant. He told her this, and it was as if a truce had finally been established. It was like yes, yes, *yes*!

Though Richard knew that a pregnancy would only complicate his situation even further, he was committed after that to ensuring that his life and that of his lover could not be so easily disentangled. He left Sofie's apartment that night with a heady and euphoric sensation, as if everything had been resolved. When he knew, in fact, that nothing was ever likely to be resolved.

Sofie bathed alone while Richard shaved. It was almost dark by the time they got back to Gibb's Farm and they were both very hungry. Watching him shave, Sofie placed her hands on her belly. She didn't know how she could ever forgive him for having wanted to make her pregnant and then, when it finally happened, a couple of years later—even if it *was* an accident—for having convinced her to deny what had already been set in motion and get rid of the embryo, by claiming merely that the timing wasn't right.

Richard stood at the mirror with a towel wrapped around his waist, his hair still wet from the shower, scraping the stubble off his face with neat meticulous downward strokes of the razor. Oblivious, it seemed, to anything Sofie might be thinking.

Once, while she was at Sarah Lawrence, Sofie had bought a packet of razor blades and tried to slit her wrist. But she had failed to press down hard enough to draw more than token blood. At the time she was surprised by how impossible it had been to press down any harder, by her unacknowledged reluctance to actually pull it off. She was both dismayed and awed by the stubborn resistance of her tendons, which seemed to have been designed to protect the delicate blue veins from the trembling blade of the razor she had held in her hand.

When she said to Zuri, in Swahili, that yes, she did speak a bit of the language—*Ndiyo, ninazungumza Kiswahili kidogo*—Zuri smiled, almost blissfully, and, lifting his chin to gaze out at the sea, where Richard was diving among the coral reefs, he said, "Ni siku nzuri sana!"

Sofie had to ask him to repeat what he had just said. "Nini?"

But once she understood she laughed, and said in English, "Why, yes, it is a beautiful day. Isn't it?"

→ ⇢ ⇻ ⇥➔

They sat together at the same cozy table near the window, with the same red candle in a brass saucer burning between them. But the window was darkened now. The coffee fields were no longer visible, and the leopards that roamed these hills were already on the prowl.

"I know it was disappointing for you not to have seen any of the big cats," said Richard. "But I'm sure we'll see plenty of them in the Serengeti."

"You were disappointed too. Weren't you?"

"I don't know," he said, lifting his glass and swirling the malbec. He was struck by the intrusive thought that only the most full-bodied wines looked anything at all like blood. "It might be better sometimes not to see everything that's going on."

"What does that mean?" said Sofie. She held her knife and fork poised over her plate and looked at him while the silence between them stretched, and stretching, grew more treacherous.

Finally she set the silverware down and said, "I thought you were the head-on guy? The one who never wanted to look away?"

Richard wasn't even sure what he'd meant by what he'd just said. But he realized that he might have made a mistake, and revealed more of what he had on his mind than he had intended to do.

Or was this one of those instances of unintentionally saying precisely the one thing that most needed to be said? Whether or not you wanted to say it.

"I'm sorry, I wasn't referring to—"

"You don't have to apologize," said Sofie. "Not again."

She turned her head to look out the window through which nothing could be seen. Her face was reflected in the dark glass, but it was her profile that Richard was staring at.

"There's no need for any of that," she said, barely moving her lips. "Not anymore."

For the rest of that meal they sat opposite each other, close enough to have touched, had either of them been inclined to do so.

When they got back to the room Richard stoked the fire. He regarded the quickening blaze with something bordering on desperation. He could hear Sofie in the bathroom, which was also open to the heat of the flames, getting ready for bed. Her movements now were practiced, automatic, practically mechanical. And he knew that if he tried to make love to her on this last night at Gibb's Farm she would respond in the same way: automatically, mechanically, and with about as much enthusiasm for the lovemaking as she must feel when she applied cold cream to her face.

Assuming she wouldn't reject him outright by saying, "No! I don't want you to touch me. Leave me alone!" And after that, turn her back on him.

Once the fire was crackling again Richard sat on the edge of the bed, and stared at his feet. Earlier, having excused himself to go to the restroom, he'd listened—while standing over the toilet trying to determine whether his urine was getting any lighter or darker—to a message on his cell phone.

His son Robert had called to tell him about a trophy he'd won in that summer's regional tennis tournament. The boy's voice sounded so near and dear in Richard's ear, so clear and breathless with pride. "I aced him seven times," he said. "Seven times!"

The boy was so pleased with himself that Richard couldn't detect any regret that his father hadn't been there to watch him lift the trophy.

Robert had real talent, that's what all the pros said. And Richard was determined to spare no expense or effort in order to enable his son to realize his potential. But he knew—despite Dr. Boehnert's assurances—that he probably wouldn't be around to see how far young Robert could go with his talents.

II

To get around the Ngorongoro Crater they had to circumvent the crater's rim. That meant driving down from Gibb's Farm and back up the same way they'd gone the day before, towards the entrance to the crater, following the narrow road that snaked up the mountainside and tunneled through the dense lush forest that carpeted the crater's southeastern flank. It was foggy, and cold inside the Land Rover. Until they came out on the western side of the crater and the woodlands suddenly grew sparse before falling away altogether. Then they were rumbling along a straight banging unpaved road that sloped down into the most barren and desolate landscape Sofie had ever seen.

They were entering the territory, according to the research she had done, where man had begun. Olduvai—or more correctly, Oldupai—Gorge wasn't far from here, and neither was Laetoli. She and Richard had talked about a side trip to these sites, but there was the time constraint, and he had convinced her that she would be better off focusing on the living rather than the dead, that readers would be much more interested in some kind of wildlife narrative than a rehashing of antiquated anthropological speculation.

"This road," called Mwenge, with a backward glance at the two of them, as another overcrowded and dust-shrouded bus flashed by, battering the Land Rover with its wake, "goes all the way from Arusha to Mwanza. On the shores of Lake Victoria."

Although this was once—millions of years ago—a Garden of Eden, Sofie saw no sign of life out there. Not even a lone thorn tree beneath that sky of diaphanous and widely scattered clouds. Nothing but the hard flat baked earth. And the occasional Maasai warrior in the deep distance, carrying a long stick and wearing only his bright red *shuka*, walking like someone out of a Beckett play—as if he were in no hurry, and going nowhere—alongside his straggling herd of gaunt and hump-necked cattle.

Sofie wondered about these men, what their lives were like, what their women were like, and where they might have come from. And what glaring necessity could possibly force them to wander hatless beneath such a bold and merciless sun—a sun Mwenge had said was capable of frying the brain of a Thomson gazelle, hence the evolution of a configuration of arteries and veins in a sinus cavity at the base of the gazelle's skull called the carotid rete which was designed to keep its brain cooler than the rest of its body, even when the gazelle was running for its life—in search of what could only be, at most, a few desiccated leaves, or a cup of brackish water. If any terrain deserved the epithet of hostile, it had to be this one.

But now that she was no longer as tender inside—or was it only resentment and regret that had made her resist Richard for so long?—Sofie was beginning to feel up to the challenge of the rough travel. And not only that, but she was beginning to enjoy the thrill of the journey as well.

The constant jolting of the Land Rover was, though, drearily brutal. And the noise so deafening that she couldn't have heard anything Richard said, unless she leaned close to his lips.

But Richard wasn't saying anything. Instead he was practically grimacing, as he stared out the side window at all that bright nothingness.

21

It had heated up quickly inside the Land Rover. And the billowing tails of grit and dust attached to every car or truck they passed, going either way, made it impossible to keep the windows open. Sofie closed her eyes and remembered what it was like to lie on the beach at Pemba, with the breeze off the sea cooling her, while she listened to the rhythmic sighing of the surf.

Zuri had apologized profusely, at first, for disturbing her. He kept saying that he was very sorry for interrupting her. But the van wasn't his, he knew nothing about engines, and it was the first time he had been entrusted with the vehicle. Maybe all it needed was some petrol? If she could lend him enough money to fill the jerry can he'd be on his way. The petrol station wasn't that far. He could walk there and back. And if he was lucky he wouldn't be too late, and he wouldn't get into too much trouble. And he could pay her back tomorrow.

All the cash that she and Richard had between them—both the *shilingi* and the dollar bills, in denominations greater than twenty, and printed after 2007—was in the money belt that Richard had placed in the safe in their bungalow, before joining the diving party at the dock. Richard had tried to hide his disappointment at Sofie's decision to stay behind on the beach, rather than come along for a ride in the boat. But she had wanted to be alone, and he said he understood. Though she didn't believe he could imagine that all she really wanted to do was lie there on the warm sand and think of nothing.

Although the sea was calm that day, Sofie had said that she was afraid that the rocking of the boat might make her nauseous again. In parting Richard had delicately touched her forearm.

It was hard for him to measure and determine just how much worse the pain was now than it had been before they got in the Land

Rover and left Gibb's Farm that morning. Mwenge drove like a man possessed, like a character out of the renegade world of Mad Max. Why was he always in such a goddamned hurry? And so insistent upon overtaking everything that moved in front of them? And so serenely oblivious too, of how fast they were going? It wasn't as if anything that was waiting for them out there was going to go away, was it?

The traditional pace of change in this land was that of millennia. The sun rose and set, just like it had always done, and that was all. Time here was measured not by the numbers on the face of a clock, nor even by the heartbeats or lifetimes of individuals, but by geological standards.

The violent shuddering of the Land Rover as the tires furiously pounded the stony road that was so rarely graded made Richard's back feel like it was being wrenched open from within. It was as if his spine were composed of rusty sockets that were being torn loose by the force of the jarring of metal.

What had started as an acute, localized throbbing—something he had hoped to prevent with the Oxycodone; and if not, the Tramadol tablet that he had in his pocket—kept seeping outward, like some viscous or molten liquid oozing through a narrow funnel and spreading throughout his lower back, where it hardened and finally cracked under the unrelenting pressure of the shimmying vibrations of the Land Rover. Richard wanted to scream. Or command Mwenge to take his foot off the accelerator. But he was afraid to quit gritting his teeth.

"Are you okay?" said Sofie.

There was real concern in her green eyes. And it was precisely this that Richard had hoped to avoid.

"It's my back," he groaned, through clenched teeth. "I twisted it. While diving."

Richard's one true friend—someone he hadn't gone to college with, but instead had met when Andrea insisted, within a year of the birth of the twins, when both of them were seriously considering ending their marriage, that they see someone, a therapist—had told Richard that there was a difference between 'black,' or outright, and 'white,' or more innocent, lies.

"Withholding essential information is often," Dr. Weber had said, "as destructive in terms of its many unpredictable repercussions as making a statement that you know to be false." But there were times, he explained, when the withholding of information was justified. The problem being that in order to justify such omissions one had to do so solely in response to the needs of the person from whom the truth was being withheld. And the determination of that person's needs—independent of any egotistical considerations of one's own—was rarely possible.

"Do you want to lie down?" said Sofie.

Without waiting for Richard to answer her question she got up and went to the back of the Land Rover. Mwenge had told them stories about getting stuck during the rainy season—when the roads crossing the most apparently innocuous of streams, all of which were dry now, were often washed out with flash flooding—and of having to spend a freezing night huddled inside the Rover, praying that the water wouldn't rise any higher. Wool blankets were as essential as the pair of spare tires bolted to the back door and they were stored in the cargo niche, along with the duffel bags and other supplies. Sofie found two blankets, and spread one of them across the last row of three seats. Then she folded the other blanket into a pillow.

Richard had turned around to watch her, bracing himself with both arms as he gripped the tubular frames of the seatbacks on opposite sides of the aisle. The muscles and tendons of his arms and shoulders were straining as they tried to absorb and counter the ceaseless shaking of the Land Rover. He felt like he was engaged in a battle of his will against that of the circumstances—a struggle between flesh and metal, man and machine, the sort of trial no human being could hope to endure for long—with the sweat streaming down his face and dripping off his chin.

When Sofie finished folding the second blanket into a pillow she turned around and looked at him and it was the most subtle of gestures, that characteristic biting of one side of her lower lip, that broke his fucking heart.

By the time they reached the entrance to the Serengeti—nothing but a crooked wooden sign hanging over the unpaved road, suspended from a pair of beams angled to suggest a roof, announcing the 'Serengeti National Park'—Richard was delirious. They had come too far by then, said Mwenge, to turn around and go back. "It is quicker now to the camp."

Sofie sat in one of the seats in front of the back row and, using bottled drinking water, she kept wetting and applying a damp handkerchief to Richard's forehead. She had never before had the opportunity to care for him like this, and it made her feel as if the bond between them was everything that Richard had always said it was: undeniable, irrevocable, everlasting.

But undermining this deeply gratifying sensation of being bound to—and caring for—the man she loved, was a current of fear. And panic with regard to his well-being. Not to mention her own fate.

Richard's face was very pale. There was no color at all in his chapped lips. His breathing was shallow, and ragged. Sofie was afraid he might not make it.

Despite Mwenge's calm, he was little comfort to her. He drove as fast as ever, no more, no less it seemed. And with that same bewitchingly impassive demeanor.

But Sofie had seen something in his eye, when he finally pulled over at the entrance to the Serengeti to ask what was wrong. It wasn't the sort of panicked concern she might have expected from someone entrusted with the safety of a *Mzungu* that she had seen. But neither was it resignation. Instead it was more like a profound and respectful acceptance of whatever it was that fate had in store for them.

←₊₊ ←₊₊ ←₊₊ ←

Mwenge had immediately radioed ahead to let the crew at the permanent camp site know what was going on. When he finally skidded to a stop in front of the central *nyumba*, and the plume of dust that had been trailing them ever since they entered the Serengeti overtook and enveloped them, the entire staff of a dozen men were on hand, speaking to each other in such urgent and frenzied voices that Sofie heard only gibberish. And that one word—*mgonjwa*, *mgonjwa*—repeated over and over again.

"Yeye ni mgonjwa sana!" they said, with what seemed like some sort of hysterical reverence for the fact that the white man was very very sick.

The confusion was such that they couldn't decide at first whether to try to lift Richard over the row of the three seats he was lying on, and out the back of the Land Rover. Or somehow carry him down the narrow aisle that was so cramped that even one person alone had to shuffle their feet—while stooping—to move down and out the side door.

"Oh, God!" moaned Sofie. "Oh, God!"

She felt worse than useless now, and impatient too, unable to stand still. She kept squeezing the sweat-dampened handkerchief she was clutching in her fist, while she stared wild-eyed at the backs of these muscular and well-intentioned black men who, like her, were dealing with a crisis they had not been prepared for.

It was finally deemed too difficult to lift Richard and pass him out the back of the Land Rover, so they had to get him down the aisle. Two men lay on their backs in the aisle, head to foot, with their knees bent, while two more crouched at Richard's head and feet, and four others took their places in the seats on either side of the aisle, between the back row and the side door. Then they used the blanket Richard was lying on to lift him, and pass him along, taking great care to keep one hand always under his head and another under his feet and lower back, and in this almost ceremonial way they bore him—as if he were a dead man already—the short length of the Land Rover aisle, and out the side door.

Their tent—or *nyumba*—had already been prepared, and Richard was soon lying on the one bed where Sofie would sleep by his side (even if he died, she told herself, she would remain there and sleep by his side) that night. The many zippered flaps of the tent were adjusted so that no direct sunlight poured in. Sofie could feel the weight of the equatorial sunshine that had already accumulated on the roof of the tent—like a crown of heat—but the tent was designed in such a way as to allow a pocket of air at the top of the tent to vent that heat, and lessen that weight.

Mwenge assured her that a doctor had been sent for, and was on his way. "He will determine what to do next."

Mwenge said this to her in English, and Sofie was grateful to him for that delicate consideration. It took all she had left in her to say to him, "Thank you, Mwenge. Asante sana. Thank you."

→ →→ →→⟩ →→⟩

Several hours went by, during which Richard lay as if comatose, while Sofie tried to cool his forehead and reduce the fever with the application of wet towels dipped in a bucket of melted ice. She had grown weary of asking Mwenge when the doctor would get there. Every time she ducked through the flap of the tent and asked him again—he stood outside, as if on guard, and wouldn't even sit down at the little wooden table where Sofie might have written in her journal—he said, "Very soon," without meeting her eyes.

"He is on his way," he assured her. "He will not be long."

Then he continued gazing at the empty dirt road that cut across the plains, beside which a group of giraffe were browsing on the leaves of the flat-top acacias.

Eventually Richard's eyelids fluttered open. The look in his jaundiced eyes was that of a man who did not have any idea of where he might be. But the worst of the delirium seemed to have passed. Resting in the bed seemed to be doing him good.

It occurred to Sofie to ask Richard if he thought one of those prescription pills in the bottles she'd discovered might help. She didn't know what else to do. And she was too distraught to worry about any consequences of her having poked about in his toiletry bag.

"Tramadol," he said.

Sofie struggled a bit with the child-proof cap, she was so nervous and excited to be able to do something. But she finally got it open. She helped Richard sit up enough so that he wouldn't choke on the pill and the bottled spring water that she offered him. Then she eased him back down, and sat on the bed beside him holding his hand, and stroking the loose strands of hair off his glistening forehead.

She had decided to tell him about Zuri. She didn't want Richard to die, and not know how tempted she had been to make love to the other man, while Richard went out to dive every morning. How bitter—and vengeful—she had felt at the loss of what would have been their child. How much she had wanted that child, and how hurt she had been by Richard's insistence that she abort. How much she craved the inseverable bond between them that a child, their son or daughter, would have represented. She wanted Richard to know that she had lied when she'd said she just didn't feel up to going out on the boat, that all she had wanted, every morning of those last five days on the island, was to lie alone on the beach and wait for Zuri to show up.

But she was afraid that Richard was still too weak, and not conscious enough, to hear her confession. So she decided to wait.

Although Sofie no longer feared that Richard might never open his eyes again, she could feel—through his hand in hers, and the way the tension in his fingers simply dissolved—how easily and smoothly he kept drifting away from her, every time he closed his eyes again.

It was late in the afternoon when the doctor—a short, spare, and very dark black man wearing a khaki bush shirt and long trousers—came into the tent, where the daylight was already ebbing, carrying a scuffed leather bag.

Richard's eyes were half-open and without moving or acknowledging the visitor in any way he considered the doctor's small round head, with its tiny ears and deeply creased brow, and the sparse beard of short curly white hairs that covered his face.

Sofie stood up and moved away from the bed and Mwenge, who had followed the doctor into the tent, switched on the dim lights that were powered by the solar panel batteries.

"He's much better now," said Sofie.

The doctor nodded his head, while keeping his eyes trained on Richard.

Richard made a move to sit up and the doctor lifted a hand and said, "There's no need for that."

"I'd like to sit up," said Richard, with a little more belligerence than he had intended. "I've been lying on my back all day."

Sofie helped rearrange the pillows behind him while the doctor looked around for some place to set his bag down. The bedside table was too small, so he finally handed the bag to Mwenge.

"What took you so long?" said Richard, voicing precisely the same complaint that Sofie had had in mind.

"A flat tire," said the doctor. "And no good spare."

"You're kidding," said Richard. "No spare? Out there?"

29

"I wish I were kidding," said the doctor.

"He could have—"

But Richard silenced Sofie with a stern glance, to keep her from saying the rest of it.

"You're right," said the doctor, looking at her in that penetrating way he had of immediately sizing everything up, and making a quick and informed judgment. "If it would have been fatal, I would be certifying your husband's death right now."

Richard snorted at that, but the residue of pain that still plagued his lower back made him wince and cough. Sofie didn't know what he could possibly be scorning, but she was instantly beside him, trying to help.

"Would you like a cup of tea?" said the doctor, speaking to both of them. "I'm assuming that neither of you have had anything to eat since you got here? And only water to drink?"

Before Sofie could answer for Richard the doctor said to Mwenge, "Je, utaleta chai na vikombe vitatu tafadhali?"

→ →→ →→ →→→

Once the tea had been served Dr. Bukuku asked Sofie if she would mind if he spoke to Richard in private. He had formally introduced himself while waiting for Mwenge to return with the tea tray, explaining that he had been fortunate enough to have studied in London during the late seventies, as a Commonwealth Professional Fellow, at the end of which time he was hired and interned at The Royal Marsden Hospital for another three years before deciding to return to Tanzania and dedicate himself to helping the rural poor.

Sofie looked at Richard, who merely gestured with his eyebrows, as if to say, "I don't have a clue what he wants."

"Perhaps that man"—referring to Mwenge, who still stood dutifully outside the tent—"can help you arrange for some dinner to be brought here. Say, in half an hour or so?"

Before Sofie could agree the doctor called Mwenge in and explained to him in Swahili what he wanted done. Sofie reluctantly followed Mwenge to the dining tent.

"Don't worry," Mwenge said, along the way. "This doctor is a good man. He has lots of knowledge. And he doesn't want anything for it."

Richard listened to Sofie and Mwenge walk away from the tent. And then he became aware of the first of the night calls, accompanying the rapidly thickening dusk.

"Do you mind if I sit down?" said the doctor.

"Of course not."

Dr. Bukuku pulled the folding canvas chair up to the side of the bed and sat there, with his legs crossed, holding his cup of tea in both hands. He looked at Richard in a kindly way, but it was almost as if he pitied Richard.

Richard sighed, audibly, certain now that the crisis had passed. "I'm sorry to have needlessly called you out here," he said.

"Never mind that," said the doctor. "And besides, no effort is ever wasted."

Richard looked at this small man, who he couldn't figure out. He was used to making quick judgments himself, often based on first impressions and the need to know, always trusting his intuition. But this man who sat beside him as if he were simply paying a visit to a neighbor baffled him.

"You don't have to tell me what it is," said the doctor. "And I wouldn't blame you if you didn't. But I'm convinced that the symptoms that were described to me over the radio—the sweating, and delirium—are related to something that you brought with you. Rather than anything you've contracted while traveling in this country."

Richard set his cup of tea on the bedside table. He had heard

31

about men like this doctor, blessed—or cursed, depending upon how you looked at it—with some sort of gift, the ability to see what no one else could see. But he'd never dealt directly with anyone like that. All the people he knew and associated with lived with their feet and eyes on the ground, looking only as far as their next few steps. And the intuition that Richard himself relied upon was more the result of practical experience than any mystical ability to peer into someone else's soul.

"You mustn't make too much of this," cautioned the doctor. "It's just a supposition. Or, if you like, an educated guess. The pain has receded, is that right? But you know for a fact that it will be back?"

Richard leaned forward a little so that he could readjust the pillows behind his back. He glanced at the entrance to the tent, and thought it strange indeed that it had come to this.

"Am I wrong?" said the doctor, setting his cup of tea on the bedside table, next to Richard's cup.

"She doesn't know," said Richard. Adding, after that, "No one knows."

"She isn't your wife?"

When Richard didn't say anything the doctor said, "You're under no obligation to tell me anything. And I can leave if you want. It's a long drive back to Loliondo. But it's too late already to go through the Serengeti. It's not allowed, driving at night in the park. So I will be staying here with my driver. We'll be sleeping with the staff. If you need me later," and he uncrossed his legs and placed the palms of his hands on his thighs, making ready to get up, "you can ask for me at any time. All you have to do is ring that little bell."

→ →→ →→→ →→→→

Richard insisted that he felt well enough to eat in the dining tent, so Sofie rang the bell, as she had been instructed. Within minutes a member of the staff appeared with the park ranger, who carried an AK-47 with a battered wooden stock slung over one shoulder. No guests were allowed to move between the tents at night without an escort, due to the proximity of the wildlife all around them.

"It is only a precaution," Mwenge had explained. "In the dry season the animals are drawn to the water." He was referring, among other things, to the treated canvas bags that were filled upon request with fire-heated water and hoisted on pulleys located behind each tent, used to provide—via a plastic tube and the force of gravity—the water for the shower. "We cannot smell it like they do. But they can smell moisture from many kilometers away."

Richard felt weak and a little dizzy, as a result of not having eaten anything all day. But otherwise it was almost as if nothing had happened. He knew that—except for the cancerous cells attached to his pancreas—he was okay now. So he insisted not only on the presence of both Mwenge and Dr. Bukuku at their table, but on red wine with the *biriani*.

"I see," said Dr. Bukuku, once they had all sat down together, "that you're not lacking for appetite. Or good taste."

"There's nothing wrong with me," said Richard.

Sofie placed a hand on his forearm and said, "That was such a scare, though."

"I'm sorry," said Richard, turning to look at her. And everyone sitting at the table realized how sincere, and intimate, that apology was. Almost embarrassingly sincere.

"Though sicknesses have been studied for thousands of years, perhaps even tens of thousands of years, by thoroughly capable minds," said Dr. Bukuku, "there remains, surrounding every instance of even something as simple as a common bacterial infection, a great deal of mystery. Although many of these infections can be effectively eliminated with antibiotics, this isn't always the case. And even the bacteria we've known and treated for a long time keep mutating. But something else is always at work. Don't you agree?"

The question was directed not to the table but to Richard in particular, although he wasn't quite sure what the doctor was talking about. But then he thought he understood, and he practically scoffed, "Not faith?"

"The question is," said Dr. Bukuku, lifting the fork to his lips, "what do we mean by faith?"

After the meal Richard sent Mwenge to see if there was any whisky, having insisted that they all move to the bonfire and have a drink there.

"Are you sure that's a good idea?" said Sofie. "Maybe you should take it easy."

"I survived, didn't I? Don't you think we should celebrate?"

There was something he wasn't telling her, she was sure of that. She had never seen those opiates in Richard's toiletry bag before, on any of the always brief getaway trips that they had managed to make together in the past. But she too was carrying a secret, so she didn't feel as if she had much of a right to pry, or complain. Even so, the hint of belligerence in Richard's tone—which might have been attributable to his annoyance with himself for having been ill, and having frightened her so much—put her on guard.

"I don't know," she said. "I'm a little worn out."

Sofie would have preferred returning to their tent, and getting into the bed, where they could simply hold each other. Perhaps then she could find the courage to say what she wanted to say. Perhaps then—while lying in Richard's arms, after their having experienced together the fear of her losing him—he would be able to understand what she wanted to say.

Besides, it was cold at that altitude, and she was exhausted from the long forced drive. And all that unwelcome anxiety. And she knew that although the whisky sometimes sweetened Richard's tongue—when his mood was both empathetic and buoyant—there had also been times when some festering discouragement had been fortified by the alcohol, leading to the only true ugliness that they had ever experienced together.

"You run along then," he said. "Dr. Bukuku will keep me company. Won't you?"

They were standing around the table that the staff were clearing, in the muted yellow light of a couple of hurricane lamps. Sofie didn't like the way Richard was dismissing her, and so easily substituting her presence with that of the doctor. But she sensed that Richard didn't want her to be there, not now anyway. And she was too shattered by the day's events to challenge and defy him.

"You won't be long, though, will you?" she asked.

"I'll see to it," promised Dr. Bukuku, "that he turns in shortly. We could all do with an early night."

→ ⇢ ⇥ ⇥ ⟶

Once the fire had been built up by one of the staff, who expertly arranged some windfall branches and a few logs, then knelt down and blew on the glowing embers until the flames were leaping again, Richard said, "I just wanted you to know that I do have an answer to your question."

Mwenge had found an unopened bottle of Glenfiddich, but he declined the invitation to join Richard and Dr. Bukuku for a drink. Instead he and the mirthless ranger armed with the assault rifle accompanied Sofie back to her tent. Leaving Richard and Dr. Bukuku alone, sitting on a pair of folding canvas chairs, side by side, with the now snapping fire at their feet.

Far off in the inky distance a patch of sky was faintly illuminated by one of the controlled fires set by the Serengeti park rangers. They did this, Mwenge had explained, to eliminate pests like ticks, as well as tree seedlings, and to allow new grasses to grow, once the slightest sprinkling of rain fell.

"Which question was that?" said Dr. Bukuku.

The whisky went down even better than the wine, and it soothed Richard to be sitting close enough to an open fire to feel the heat on his shins, while the whisky warmed him from within. He almost regretted that he hadn't persuaded Sofie to stay. The unfamiliar constellations were pulsing in the vast southern sky, and he would have liked to be holding her hand right now, their fingers intertwined. And feeling perhaps, if only for a moment, that everything was as it should be. That everything was going to be all right.

But what he had to say he meant only to say to this man he did not know. Someone who might possibly understand, and at the same time remain completely unaffected by the information.

"I've got a small tumor on my pancreas," he said. "Just large enough to be classified as Stage 2."

After a moment of silence, during which Dr. Bukuku was obviously contemplating this fact, he asked, "Not too large yet, that it cannot be removed?"

He said this without looking at Richard. Both men continued to gaze at the little nimbus of light hovering above the burning savanna.

"As soon as we get back to the States they're going to give it a shot. The recommendation was that I stay, and blow off the trip. They couldn't be sure how fast the tumor was growing. Or whether the stress of travel might not accelerate the cancer."

"But you decided to come anyway?"

Richard drank some of the Glenfiddich which, like all whiskys, he always took neat.

"I met Sofie almost three years ago. At first it was something I didn't attach too much importance to. It was fun, of course. It was exciting. But I didn't expect to fall in love. I have two teenage kids, twins. And I thought I couldn't imagine coming home to a house where they weren't barricaded inside their bedrooms."

"What about your wife?" said Dr. Bukuku.

Richard looked into his tumbler of whisky, and swirled the

liquid. The peaty aroma mingled with that of the burning wood, and the air crisp as that of late autumn back home. It was like a whiff of nostalgia. But it was too dark to see anything, other than the glinting of firelight reflected off the fluting cut into the glass that he held in his hand.

"We've been married a long time," he said. "Almost thirty years now. The marriage has run its course. And that course is now dry."

"I see," said Dr. Bukuku.

"But this is what I wanted to say," said Richard, turning his head to face the other man. "There was another problem, before we were scheduled to come here. I had to ask Sofie to do something that she didn't want to do. Something I didn't want to do either, but had to do. And I did that because I know what the outcome of all of this is going to be."

"That's what *I* mean by faith" he said. "Certain knowledge. Not hope, for some other outcome, when you know there isn't really any hope. But the unwilling conviction, the inescapable belief, that the same thing that killed my dad will, sooner rather than later, take me as well."

Richard stared straight ahead again, into the African night.

"And it just wouldn't have been fair," he said. "To go through with it. And allow that child of ours to be born. Not fair to Sofie anyway."

Sofie wasn't quite asleep when she heard Richard raise the zipper on the flap, as silently as possible, but she wasn't fully awake either. She'd dozed off, after putting her pajamas on and snuggling under the eiderdown, and moving one of the two hot water bottles to the foot of the bed, where it soon began to warm her toes. The other hot water bottle she'd held close to her belly, eagerly absorbing its heat.

For a long time she had laid there, wondering which calls she would hear that night. And why Richard had been so keen to be left alone with Dr. Bukuku. She'd laid there thinking of how different everything could be, if only some other choice would have been made. Including the choice she'd made on the beach in Pemba.

And then she'd finally slipped into a shallow dream, that of traveling in a fast car—which might have been Richard's BMW—along a wide flat unpaved road, across a landscape with no depth of field or horizon, with the roof down, and the wind blowing in her hair.

Now she listened to Richard feel his way towards the bed in the dark. She heard him grunt, as he bent over to unlace each shoe. Then he unbelted his pants and let them fall to the floor of the tent.

Sofie lay perfectly still, as Richard inched into the bed, peeling back the eiderdown only enough to slip under it. She could smell the wood smoke in his hair, and the whisky on his breath, as he edged his body slowly, and by cautious degrees, closer to hers. Careful as he was not to make much noise and wake her, she felt certain that he hoped that she wasn't asleep.

⇢ ⇢ ⇥ ⇥⟶

Every morning, at breakfast, Mwenge would ask—after his *Habari za asubuhi?* and his *Umeamkaje?*—what animals they thought they had heard during the night. Mwenge could imitate the cough of the ostrich, the bark of the zebra, the guttural blarting—that *uunt-uunt*—of the wildebeest, as well as the giggles of the hyenas. But that morning he asked if they'd heard the lion.

Richard had fallen asleep almost immediately, after he realized that Sofie was only pretending to be asleep. But the pain in his back woke him later, in the middle of the night. And until he got up and took a couple of Oxycodone, and after that removed the hot water bottle from Sofie's hands—she was breathing audibly then, slow and steady, reassuringly—and applied it to his lower back, he had laid there thinking about what Dr. Bukuku had told him. But he never heard any lion.

"It was a male," said Mwenge. "He sounded worried. Like this."

And he opened his mouth wide and forced the air out of the bottom of his gut, almost as if he were retching. Again and again Mwenge produced a doleful and strangled huffing: *hunh, hunh, hunh.*

The staff standing around the breakfast counter laughed and applauded, encouraging Mwenge, who delighted in his audience. He seemed to have quite a reputation for performing like this.

"The lion's call can carry for eight kilometers," he said, "depending on the wind. It might have been a young male, recently forced to live on his own, who has wandered into another pride's territory. Or an old male, banished from his pride by a younger and stronger male. Either way that lion is not happy."

"Is there any chance we could find him?" said Sofie. "I mean," placing her hand on Richard's forearm, "if you're feeling up to it?"

"Where's Dr. Bukuku?" said Richard.

"He left before dawn," said Mwenge. "He runs a clinic in Loliondo, and they are always busy."

"Why don't you take Sofie," said Richard, "in search of the lion? I think I'll stay here and rest today."

← ← ← ←

"If you find him," said Richard, handing Sofie the Canon, "take lots of pictures. Won't you?"

"Of course," she said, allowing him to help her into the Land Rover, where she settled on one of the two seats closest to Mwenge, who must have sensed that something was wrong. For as soon as they said good-bye and he shifted into gear he glanced over his shoulder and began by saying, "Lions used to roam over the entire continent. Everywhere except the Sahara. And the densest regions of the Congo Basin. There are paintings of lions in caves in France. Some people believe there were lions in Spain. And Italy, too. They were definitely in Macedonia, and all across the Middle East. Even on the edges of the desert. And down through India, where only a very few remain today."

Mwenge usually provided information in appropriately timed tidbits, when they saw a particular animal or came to a place where they needed to know how to look for something, like the leopard's tail that was so hard to spot, dangling from a high branch of a Sycamore Fig. Or in his more expansive responses to their many questions. But Sofie hadn't said a word since they drove away from the camp, leaving Richard behind.

"But that is no longer the case," said Mwenge, looking at her in the rearview mirror. "Though there are lions as far west as Senegal, they now roam only a very small percentage of their historic range."

Mechanically, without any enthusiasm at all, Sofie opened her journal to a blank page. But after noting the date she only made a pretense of writing down the things that Mwenge was telling her.

→ →⟩ →⟩ →⟩

Richard watched them drive away. Then he remained standing there, in the circular track in front of the central *nyumba*, until all he could see of the Land Rover was the cloud of dust it was raising.

It was still early, the air still quite cool. But the sunshine on his face was already very warm. Eat, he thought, or be eaten, recalling something else that Dr. Bukuku had said last night. "That's the only law there is," he'd said, "anywhere."

Richard turned around and sought out the head of the staff, a short-limbed man with a scar on the side of his shaven skull, something Richard would have liked to ask him about, whether it was ceremonial, or the result of an accident. Or perhaps even a knife fight?

40

Instead he said, "Is there any way you could radio for a vehicle? Any chance I could hire a ride to Loliondo?"

As they searched for the lone male lion—and Sofie knew that Mwenge, with his preternatural talent for finding whatever he chose to look for in those endless plains, would eventually find the lion—she thought about how the entire trip had involved so much looking. And being looked at.

Ever since they arrived in Zanzibar they had been involved in this dualistic seeing. Though Tanzanians were accustomed to tourists—all of whom they referred to collectively as Europeans, or *Wazungu*, at least so long as they were light-skinned—just as soon as she and Richard had crossed Creek Road and walked beyond the limits of Stone Town, entering *Ng'ambo*, or the 'Other Side,' they were being watched. And stared at openly, with that peculiar blend of inquisitive nonchalance and apparent innocence, that almost languid and unconcerned scrutiny, that could easily be mistaken for indifference. Or perhaps even repressed hostility.

Sofie tried to avoid blatantly staring at the things she saw, at the people who were staring at her, at the beautiful *kangas* the women wore, and the skinny legs and bare feet of the children dressed in rags, at the dilapidated Soviet-style apartment blocks, and beyond these the overcrowded zinc-roofed cinderblock shacks so many families lived in. And all that trash—both man-made and biodegradable—casually strewn by the sweep of the rushing rain waters in open ditches that functioned as culverts. But since everything she and Richard were seeing was so new to them, and so often unexpected, it was hard to look away. Because Sofie wanted to *see*, everything.

Despite the latent hostility that might have lurked in the eyes of some of the more religious men, Sofie had never felt threatened, not even once. Not even when she was alone with Zuri. She had never felt any overt animosity directed towards either her or Richard, none whatsoever. Which was a bit hard to understand, given the way the *Wazungu*—and the Arabs before them, as Richard had pointed out—had long ravaged the continent, pilfering its ivory and gold, and murdering and enslaving so many of its people.

But it was the same way in the parks, where all the animals—both predators and prey—were constantly involved in a game of looking. Whether it was zebra or wildebeest or elephant or roan antelope. Or a pair of tiny dik-dik—the small antelope that mate for life—hoping to remain hidden among the scant foliage of a desiccated bush. Just as soon as any animal was spotted, just as soon as the lens of the Canon was extended and zoomed in on its target, there they were: a pair of alert living eyes, staring right back at Sofie.

Richard sat at the little table outside the tent and waited patiently for his ride. He sat facing the hills to the west, with the swiftly rising sun warming his neck and shoulders. It was a moment of peace—what might have been real peace, if only he weren't condemned to consider the fact, again and again, that he was most likely dying—during which he tried not to be unrealistic.

Dr. Bukuku had told him that this man—whose difficult name he had written down for Richard—was an eighty year old former priest of the Lutheran Church who'd had a vision. In the vision Ambilikile Mwasapile was informed that he could work wonders using the roots of the *mgamriaga*, or poison arrow, tree. So he went into the bush—where he followed the visionary instructions he had received—and distilled a potion that thousands of Kenyans and Tanzanians had come to drink in the hopes of ridding themselves of all sorts of chronic conditions, including AIDS, ulcers, diabetes and high blood pressure. And even cancer.

Dr. Bukuku said that people used to come by the truckload to drink this potion out of tin mugs that were served to them directly out of the hands of the former pastor. They were charged five hundred Tanzanian shillings—less than twenty-five cents—for the privilege of drinking something that many believed could save their lives. Of those five hundred *shilingi* Ambilikile Mwasapile kept only one hundred for himself. The remaining four hundred were split between his helpers and the Lutheran Church.

"There were so many people who wanted to drink this potion that the man could have become rich. He could have built a palace, like many African leaders have done. But instead he uses his share of the money to prepare the potions, while he continues to live in a mud hut. And every day he serves this drink himself, from 7:00 a.m. to 7:00 p.m."

Dr. Bukuku said that even cabinet ministers and celebrities—including the wife of the president of the DCR, Joseph Kabila—had come to Loliondo, often in helicopters, joining the craze, which reached its peak in the summer of 2011, when the Tanzanian government finally took measures to halt, or at least slow down, the seemingly endless flow of cure seekers.

"People were traveling to Loliondo in all sorts of vehicles. Anything they could find. Many of these vehicles were unsuited for the rough roads. They broke down along the way, or became stuck in the mud during the rainy season. Some people succumbed to the heat and fatigue, and died of whatever ailed them while waiting in line. In addition to that there was too much stress on the very limited infrastructure of our town. The government did not prohibit anyone from coming to Loliondo, but they did undertake a campaign to convince people of the difficulties involved in making the trip. They said that they could not guarantee that there would be enough food and water, or toilets and shelter, at Loliondo, and that people should consider this before making the trek."

Like any other fad, enthusiasm for Mwasapile's magic eventually diminished, as many people who had come to be cured died instead. The roads to Loliondo were no longer clogged with twenty-kilometer queues of sundry vehicles bearing pilgrims. But desperate people still flocked to Loliondo hoping for a miracle.

And this was because some who had been there swore that the potion had indeed saved their lives. And many others still believed that this mysterious potion could save them as well.

"That is why I asked you what you meant by faith," Dr. Bukuku had said. "Because only if you truly believe that something can work, will it happen. The power of the mind knows no limits."

Sofie gazed out the side window, without really making any effort to spot anything. There were the usual mingled herds of zebra and wildebeest, and plenty of Thomson gazelles all over the place. And a few ostrich, as well as some bush buck in the distance, the most dangerous medium-sized antelope to hunt, according to Mwenge, since bush buck will hide after being wounded and wait until the hunter—following the spoor of blood—comes in looking for his trophy, before bursting out of the bush and charging the hunter and impaling him with their sharp horns.

They had even seen three adolescent cheetahs, resting beneath a small leafless tree, less than fifty meters from a group of Tommies, who continued to graze almost as if the cheetahs weren't there. Mwenge stopped the Land Rover so that Sofie could take pictures of the cheetahs, in the foreground, calmly watching the gazelles, while the gazelles—which never quite took their eyes off the cheetahs—grazed in the background.

"So little happens," she muttered, inadvertently speaking her thoughts. "Until the moment it does happen."

"It is very important for survival," said Mwenge, "not to waste precious energy. The cheetah know how close they have to get to the gazelle to catch them."

"But why do the Tommies risk grazing so close to that tree? They could eat grass anywhere, couldn't they?"

"The cheetah are the fastest animal. But the Tommies are the next fastest. And they can cut like this"—he demonstrated a quick zigzagging motion with his hands—"much quicker than the cheetah. And they can run longer, thanks to the cooling system in their heads. As long as they can see the cats, they are always maintaining the necessary distance."

"Always?" said Sofie. She tried to imagine what it would be like to stand there at such a short distance from an animal that would like to have you for lunch.

"No, not always," said Mwenge. "Sometimes they do not calculate so good. And one mistake of judgment is all it takes. Then it is all over. Very quickly."

→ ⇢ ⇥ ⇥→

The drive to Loliondo was uneventful. The driver of the Land Rover that had come to fetch Richard was a very young man, who at first seemed a little morose. Until Richard asked him if he knew anything about Ambilikile Mwasapile.

"Oh yes," said the driver. "Ambilikile Mwasapile is a most respected man in our community. He has saved very many lives."

Richard felt like challenging him. This young driver—who had the face of a boy, and might not have been all that much older than Robert, who would also be driving a car in a couple of years, whether or not Richard was around to help him learn how to do it—could not possibly know for a fact that Mwasapile had actually saved any lives. Could he?

"How do you know?"

The driver glanced at Richard in the rearview mirror and said, "Do you know Revelations? 22:1? Then the angel showed me the river of the water of life," he quoted, practically singing the words, "as clear as crystal, flowing from the throne of God!"

Confidently gripping the steering wheel with both hands, the guileless driver continued to concentrate on the dirt track they were following across the sere empty plain.

"I know," said the young man, with more self-assurance than Richard might have expected or deemed justified, "because I have been told. And I have seen," he added, "with my own eyes, what miracles Babu can perform."

"Do you know for a fact," said Richard, "that he has cured anyone of cancer?"

"Kansa?" said the driver, using the Swahili word. "Oh yes, most certainly. Babu always cures every kansa."

They stopped near a kopje and ate their packed lunch together, Mwenge remaining in the driver's seat while Sofie sat in the seat behind him. Sometimes she felt like there was a glass wall between them, and this always reminded her of what it had been like with Zuri. Especially when he reached out and touched her naked thigh for the first time, his fingertips light as the tread of a caterpillar.

As soon as the memory came to her Sofie shook it out of her head. She was tired of sitting in the Land Rover, and would have liked to get out and stretch her legs. But Mwenge said that it wasn't allowed.

"In the Serengeti it is prohibited to walk without a research permit. No walking safaris are allowed. But where we are staying, just outside of the park boundary, you are free to go anywhere you want. As long as you go with the guard."

Sometimes it was hard for Sofie to imagine that there was anything out there to really worry about. Just as she hadn't worried about any of the things that she probably should have worried about with Zuri.

But that was because they hadn't seen any of the violence of life in the Serengeti. They hadn't seen any kills, for example, and the landscape reminded her so very much of Spain, where she had studied abroad. Or some of the semi-arid parts of the Southwestern United States. Change the trees, she thought, and it might be another part of the world where man's presence had long ago decimated—or at least controlled—the greatest threats to his life.

But she knew—like a fact in a book, with no visceral certainty attached to the knowledge, nothing she could *feel* anyway—that if she set out and started walking across that plain she would come, sooner or later, across an animal that would look at her and see nothing more than her flesh and bones. Which was all Zuri had seen.

The road they were following to Loliondo was gullied with deep ruts cut by the rains—and on top of that, perhaps, the pounding the red clay had taken from all that pilgrim traffic coming from Kenya—forcing the driver to carefully negotiate the deep scars in the broken earth. As he did so the Land Rover rocked and leaned precariously, to one side or the other. But even when the traction was lost for a moment, and the wheels briefly spun, the Land Rover plunged forward, carrying on towards its destination.

Already Richard had seen several abandoned cars, stripped of their wheels, with the hood and trunk lifted like a pair of outstretched arms. But some of the abandoned vehicles were intact, and just sitting there, where they had come to a halt and their drivers had given up, under the blazing equatorial sun.

"Do many people still come," asked Richard, "to see Pastor Mwasapile? And drink his magic potion?"

"Ndiyo," said the driver, nodding his head enthusiastically, and forgetting for a moment that Richard didn't speak Swahili.

Richard looked at the rusting metal carcasses that littered the roadside the same way those bones that the hyenas didn't find and devour—making their feces white—must litter the Serengeti plains.

"So where are the long lines?"

"Are we going to see Mchungaji Mwasapile?" asked the driver, glancing at Richard in the rearview mirror. He was genuinely confused. "Or the clinic? Je, I am told you want to visit Dr. Bukuku?"

←↞ ←↞ ←↞ ←

After lunch they drove around, past the stretch of blackened savannah still smoldering from the controlled fire Mwenge had pointed out from camp the previous evening, searching for the lion he was so determined to find. While they continued to look for this one lion, Mwenge kept providing Sofie with all sorts of curious facts that she noted more out of a sense of obligation to his pride in his knowledge than any genuine interest she had in remembering anything he said.

Because she couldn't imagine what she might be able to make out of all of this. Who, for example, would be interested in buying something she wrote about an adulterous safari in Tanzania? And how could she honestly tell that story anyway? Or that of the possibly futile search for one lone male lion in the northern Serengeti?

Mwenge didn't even know for sure that this lion had recently been driven out of its pride, and was now roaming in another pride's territory. He didn't know that the lion was old and perhaps ill, or in some other way disoriented and disturbed, and therefore especially vulnerable and unpredictable.

Mwenge had only heard the lion's call during the night. The rest of it was pure fantasy.

→ ↠ ↠ ↠→

"Yes," said Richard, "it's Dr. Bukuku I want to see. Of course. But I'm just curious, that's all. I think I'd like to see where the pastor lives. And how he treats all these people who still come to him hoping to be cured."

The young driver thought about this, as they bumped along and continued to climb the road that led to Loliondo. He reached for the radio but Richard said, "No, please. No need to tell anyone, is there? Let's just go by this place. It isn't far, is it? And anyway, we won't be long."

Then he added, more bitterly than he had intended, "I had to wait quite a while for Dr. Bukuku yesterday. He won't mind waiting a bit for me."

When Mwenge finally said, in that calm and authoritatively hushed voice—"Pale! Pale! Kuna simba!"—and Sofie saw him, stalking a loose grouping of Cape buffaloes, her pulse quickened. She felt as if she had been shaken awake from a dull mid-afternoon doze, the result of fatigue and heat and even boredom, and found herself standing on the ledge of a waterfall. To so suddenly come upon this handsome male lion, with his thick dark mane, walking all by himself across the Serengeti plain, his huge feet padding, as if he, like those Maasai herdsmen she had seen, was in no hurry at all: it almost took her breath away.

The lion was simply trailing along, behind the herd of big black bulls, at a distance that both parties seemed to accept. The buffaloes trudged ahead, with certain individuals among them stopping to flick their tails and drop their heads to graze a bit, while others turned their entire massive bodies around so that they could look back at the lion, which made no effort at all to conceal its steady approach.

There it is again, thought Sofie. That unperturbed, noncommittal, and mutual staring. Both predator and prey silently considering each other. Almost as if the other formed part of the landscape. Which was, in fact, the case.

"He is definitely hungry," said Mwenge, rolling cautiously

forward. The herd of buffaloes were spread out and thinned, further ahead, following a game trail that looked like it might eventually cross the dirt track that Mwenge was following. Neither the lion nor the buffalo took any notice of the Land Rover that was flanking them.

"And I do not think," said Mwenge, "that he is pleased to be so hungry. And so alone."

The town of Loliondo sat in a river valley surrounded by low wooded hills, and it turned out that Ambilikile Mwasapile lived in an even smaller village, called Samunge, which was somewhere up in those hills. The driver of the Land Rover, whose name was Isamael, took some convincing—which included the offer of a crisply folded fifty dollar bill—to agree to make the journey into the hills. And especially to agree not to radio in and let Dr. Bukuku—who had sent the Land Rover for Richard—know what he was doing.

But Richard assured Isamael that he only wanted to see for himself what all the fuss had been about. As they drove into the hills, along a gouged and dusty road bordered increasingly now by tropical trees—among which were telltale amounts of trash, all sorts of scraps and shreds and broken things impossible to identify and not flammable enough to burn—Isamael kept talking about the height of Babu's popularity, back in 2011, when some people who had made the trip from Arusha, which was usually an eight hour drive, had to wait in line for seven days to get a drink of the potion that was constantly being brewed in huge vats over open fires.

"Many thousands of sick people," he said, as if to prove that what he'd been saying all along was true, "drink from the same cup. Every day, for so many days. But no one ever gets sick from drinking from the same cup."

Richard looked out the side window at the abandoned cars and minivans, skeletal ruins rusting among the luxuriant green of the banana trees. He had already noticed how conscientious everyone in the camps had been about personal hygiene, insisting upon the *washi*—when a member of the staff would stand behind a small table with an enamel basin resting upon it, offering first one pitcher of soapy water, and then another of unsoaped water, for the rinsing of your hands—before you entered the dining tent. Until now he hadn't even considered the risks of putting his lips to a tin mug that had been served to people dying from all sorts of diseases, some of which might have been contagious.

"Scientists do not know everything," said Mwenge, in that measured way he had of explaining the mysteries of nature. "And there is some disagreement about how to read the mane of a lion. But usually the dark full mane is a better mane. It means a strong, and confident, lion. And the simba wa kike always prefer a dark mane. So those genes get passed on."

Sofie was absorbed in watching the way the lion steadily closed the distance between it and the last straggling buffalo without— apparently—making much effort to do so. And the way this last huge black bull kept stopping to turn around and look back at the lion, pivoting on its forefeet and swiveling its hind feet until they were positioned between him and the rest of the herd of Cape buffaloes.

"This male has been run out of his pride," said Mwenge, who had a second, smaller, pair of binoculars that he had stopped the Land Rover to peer through.

Sofie would have thought that that last bull wouldn't want to waste any time catching up with the rest of the herd. But instead it would just stand there for a moment and stare without blinking at the approaching lion. Before finally ducking its head and turning its back on the lion and skipping forward a few steps. After which it continued to trot in the direction of the rest of the herd.

"He is a defeated outcast," said Mwenge. "Just like those bulls he is pursuing."

→ ⇢ ⇥ ⇥⟶

When Richard told the man he had come to consider to be more of a friend than a therapist—Dr. Weber, whom Richard soon started calling by his first name, Jack—about Sofie, Jack listened patiently to Richard's description of what it was like to spend time with her, of how lovely it was to have her on his arm, of how rejuvenated and recharged he felt, and how excited he was about making love again. Richard said all the usual stupid things, about feeling so much more alive than he had felt in such a very long time, all of which he—Richard—recognized as typical, and unremarkable. Even cliché perhaps. But no less real, emotionally, for being cliché.

"The thing is," he said, "it's hard for me to imagine where this will all lead."

Jack stroked his beard—a mannerism that had seemed to Richard at first both calculated and pretentious—and said, "I don't think any woman ever enters into a relationship that is at all potentially meaningful to her without imagining some sort of future with her lover. Do you?"

⟵⇤ ⇤⟵ ⇠ ←

Sofie knew that something exciting was about to happen, and her excitement made it difficult for her to register everything Mwenge was saying. She was standing in the Land Rover, with her elbows propped on the top of the roof, the Canon hanging by its strap from her neck, using Mwenge's best pair of binoculars to move back and forth between the faces of the two animals destined for what might possibly become a mortal confrontation.

"As you know," said Mwenge, his silky and melodious voice

rising out of the cabin of the Land Rover, "lions usually hunt together."

But this lion seemed so unconcerned about being alone. He walked with his mouth hanging open, his jaw relaxed, his pink tongue lolling between his incredible canines. While the bull rhythmically nodded its heavy head as it lumbered forward and, whenever it stopped and turned around, extended its wet nostrils in an effort to use the scent of the lion to get a better idea of exactly where the predator might be.

"They depend upon teamwork," said Mwenge, his voice resonating below. "Especially when confronted with such a large prey."

Sofie had the binoculars trained on the lion when—without the slightest alteration to the expression on its face—it started loping after the buffalo. She swung the binoculars back towards the bull and had a little trouble spotting him at first, due to the trembling of her hands. But then she saw that the bull had reeled away from the lion with a dip of its huge neck, and was now trotting more briskly towards the rest of the herd.

→ →→ →→→ →→→→

As they drove past a scattering of thatch-roofed huts, framed with sticks and fleshed with cracked mud, the evidence of what had happened here became undeniable. Everywhere Richard looked there were mountains of partially-incinerated trash and the remains of innumerable camp fires and other indications of the hordes of people who had once gathered here. All the roadside vegetation was trampled and pulverized. There were even signs of some barracks humor, including a lopsided plank of wood hacked in the form of an arrowhead that pointed at a path that led to the woods, upon which was written, in white chalk, "Loo with a View."

But there were no lines anymore, no one was around. Even the inhabitants of the mud huts remained invisible.

Before they reached the center of the village, Richard did see two men working in the shade of a tree, one of whom was using a crowbar to pry the rubber sidewall over the rim of a bus-sized wheel, while the other used a bicycle pump to inflate the tire of a car. The man with the handle of the bicycle pump in his hands paused and stared at Richard, as Richard cruised by in the Land Rover, with an expression that was more haunted than curious.

"There is not so much business now," said Isamael, sadly, as if he regretted the fact. "But you cannot imagine how much business is made here then. Some people come from as far as Dar es Salaam for the kikombe cha maisha. And after they drink this water of life they stay to make profit. Why not? They call their family and tell them to bring anything they can fit in one car and sell. Trucks bring everything, not only people. One bottle of Kilimanjaro brand water cost more than 2,000 shilingi! Maybe three, four times what you pay in Arusha or Mwanza. You can buy anything here then. Anything! If only you have the shilingi."

Richard wasn't appalled by the profiteering. It only made sense that the healing tourism should result in a boom to the local economy. And any economic boom was bound to leave some sort of environmental footprint. As in every other case of economic expansion, some individuals would have gained, while others might have lost, that's all. But that was the way of the world. And everywhere it was the same, always.

"They make new bus routes," said Isamael, "from every city, for hundreds of kilometers. Even from Nairobi, a new bus comes every day."

Linking, thought Richard, this tiny hamlet of mud huts in the hills of Loliondo district to the rest of the world. Linking, he thought, the steadfast believers with their faith healer, the old man who continued to live humbly enough, while offering his healing art in this isolated place where, as Isamael had said, anything could be bought, even a longer life. So long as you had enough money.

Both the bull and the lion were running now, as fast as they could, though it looked so unhurried—and unreal—almost like slow motion. But it looked as well as if the bull had made that fatal mistake, and had allowed the lion to get too close to it.

The intensity of the chase seemed to have excited even Mwenge, who set his binoculars on the co-pilot's seat and shifted into gear, driving quickly but unobtrusively towards the point where the game trail the rest of the herd had been following crossed the dirt track, making it impossible for Sofie to continue watching what was happening through her binoculars.

Dropping the binoculars into the seat beside her Sofie liberated her vision from the tunnels of its lenses and saw the pair of animals—the gold and the black—against the backdrop of the burnt sienna plain. It was a stark, and beautiful, image. Dramatic too, as the bull suddenly spun to face the lion just as the lion lunged and grabbed the bull on either side of its neck, sinking its fangs into the side of its head.

"It is always exceptional," said Mwenge, in a tone of awe, "when a lone lion attacks a healthy adult buffalo."

Bracing its forelegs, the bull thrust and dipped and swung its mighty head left and right in an effort to shake itself free from the lion. But the lion held on, even as it was tossed from side to side like a rag doll, its hind feet scrabbling as the lion tried to reach far enough forward to establish another hold on the bull's body.

Then the bull stopped and just stood there, breathing so forcefully that Sofie could see the bellowing of its lungs, while the lion hung by its forepaws from the bull's neck.

Mwenge rolled to a stop, less than fifteen meters away, and cut the engine. "The buffalo wants to gore the lion," he whispered.

Now that the Land Rover was still all Sofie could hear was the tinking of its engine. And the breeze sifting through the parched knee-high grasses.

"And the lion," said Mwenge, "wants to suffocate the buffalo."

→ ⇢ ⇢ ⇢➔

As they neared the center of the village Richard saw at last the line of Land Cruisers and other appropriate vehicles, and all the people milling about, the women in their colorful *kangas*, the hatless men in long trousers and button-down shirts with stiff collars and rolled up sleeves. The crowd wasn't anywhere near as large as Richard had imagined it would be and there were no buses, or minivans, or anything but four-wheel drives anymore. And none of those cars that could be seen on any street in any city of the world that Richard had seen earlier, abandoned by the side of the road on the way to Loliondo.

He had no idea, though, how long the line in front of them might be. It was impossible to tell how far it was still to the place where Mwasapile must be dutifully serving his magic potion to those remaining devout followers who continued to make the sacrifices necessary to undertake the long hard journey to Samunge.

But he felt with great certainty that something had changed here, other than the size of the crowd. He felt, with a pang of hopelessness, that he was too late. That the moment of maximum optimism had already passed.

⇠ ⇠ ⇠ ⇠

Both animals remained immobile, and statuesque, with the lion holding on tight to the lowered head of the bull, like some sort of grotesque appendage that might have grown there. A circle of blood was forming beneath the dripping nose of the bull and Sofie was struck again by the immutable symbiosis of the relationship between predator and prey, as well as their spectacular intimacy.

"The lion can kill the buffalo in two ways," said Mwenge. "By clamping its jaws over his nostrils and mouth. Or biting the buffalo's trachea and crushing it."

These were facts the bull must know, instinctively. But it just stood there, with its forefeet planted, while the lion held on, and waited. Sofie was close enough to see the way the bull seemed to stare—with its big black eyes—at nothing now. While it did what, she wondered; consider its next move?

Finally, after catching its breath, the bull tried to get away from the lion by simply backing away and dragging the lion—which was curled on its back—across the dirt track the Land Rover had come to a stop on.

Sofie watched this unhurried yet urgent struggle, which must have occurred countless times already, and would continue to occur so long as these two animals lived within close proximity to one another. In some ways, she thought, there was nothing individual about this encounter at all.

But when she glanced around, and saw that no other tourists had gotten wind yet of what was going on here, she realized that she and Mwenge were the only two people witnessing this unique case of a timeless event.

→ ⇢ ⇥ ⇉

Isamael parked the car at the end of the line and switched off the engine. He turned to look over his shoulder at Richard and said, "Sometimes Mzungu do not have to wait so long as other people do to see Babu."

It took Richard a moment to realize that Isamael was asking for another bribe—or token of Richard's appreciation—in exchange for a hastened interview with the venerable faith healer.

Before Richard pulled out his wallet he said, "Do Mzungu get to drink the potion too? Just like other people do?"

The rest of the herd of buffaloes had stopped and turned around to watch. They were at a safe distance, the lion was no longer an immediate threat to any of them, and they could have easily carried on and forgot about the old bull and finished making their escape, putting even more distance between themselves and the only thing that could kill them out here other than age and disease, or drought and starvation. But instead they had all stopped. And now they stood, in a staggered line, with their heavy heads lowered, as if collectively considering the ongoing struggle between one of their own and their kind's worst enemy.

The bull that was still in the grip of the lion had quit backing away and come to a stop as well, taking what looked like another break. Sofie could see that the lion too was breathing heavily, and that all of the muscles in its powerful shoulders were tensed. She could see the taut tendons straining in the lion's paws. And every bloodied tear in the buffalo's hide.

Then, as if inspired by the audience that had gathered to watch, the old bull started furiously dipping and hooking its head again. It spun around and around, ducking and wheeling, in an effort to get a horn under the lion which clung fast until somehow—it happened too quickly for Sofie to see exactly what had happened— the bull was able to shake the lion free without throwing it.

Immediately the lion sought to reaffirm its grip and that was just enough of a chance for the bull to whip its head under the lion's chest and butt the lion hard into the ground, producing a fierce grunting as it did so, before swinging its head to one side and catching the lion under an arm and with the curve of its sharp horn flinging the big cat into the air.

"Oh my God!" gasped Sofie, as the beautiful lion somersaulted and crashed to the ground, bolting—just as soon as it could scramble to its feet again—out of harm's way.

While Richard waited for Isamael to come back he considered his options. As well as the new possibilities. The new reality.

The pain in his lower back had certainly become more frequent and occasionally more intense during the trip. It had started while he'd been diving off the coast of Pemba, only days after having arrived in Tanzania. The risk of an acceleration of the growth of the tumor could never have been ruled out, he knew that, and stress was always going to be a factor.

Richard had told Andrea that he was flying to Amsterdam—which was true, since the flight to Dar es Salaam had departed from Amsterdam—and from there to Berlin, to join in the final negotiations for a very lucrative deal with Deutsche Telekom. Sofie had prepared his suitcase for the trip to Tanzania while Richard had prepared at home and in full view of his wife another suitcase—the one that he left behind in Sofie's apartment—for the two weeks that he would supposedly be spending in Central Europe.

The team of specialists at the Mayo Clinic had repeatedly warned Richard that in many cases stress was the most significant—and mysterious—contributing factor in both the worsening of a patient's condition and, when absent, any improvements the patient might experience. As long, they'd said, as he insisted upon going ahead with the trip and it involved rest and relaxation—which was not only the way that Richard had presented the trip to them, but the way he himself had imagined the first real opportunity to finally spend so much uninterrupted time alone with his lover, in a place as wondrous as Zanzibar, and as fascinating as the Serengeti—the risks of aggravating his condition were minimal.

"But the risk is always there," he'd been warned. "We won't know what we're dealing with until you get back," they'd said. "And are home again."

After the bull flung the lion into the air it hesitated for a moment, unsure whether or not to charge, before it turned to run, giving the lion a chance to recover its wits and resume the chase. Both animals were racing now as fast as they could on tired legs across that dry wind-swept plain, and Sofie had the strange feeling that the confrontation had suddenly become personal. Whereas earlier it had seemed as if this was just another of the countless encounters between predator and prey, now she felt as if the fight were more about this particular bull and this particular lion.

Which was the faster of the two animals, and soon narrowed the gap between them. Enough that it could leap onto the bull again.

As soon as the bull felt the lion on its back it started spinning, in circle after circle, as it tried to clip the lion with its horns and rid itself of the pest. But once again the lion clung tightly to the bull, far enough away this time from the bull's head to avoid its horns, with one paw raking a grip behind the bull's shoulder and the other arm reaching across the bull's back while the lion's teeth were sunk near its spine.

Together the bull and the lion spun—the black and gold, the tawny gold on black—in an almost hypnotic, and dizzying, dance. Until the bull finally lost its footing and sank onto its hindquarters, exhausted again.

Isamael returned to the Land Rover and sidled in behind the wheel. "It is arranged," he said, smiling boldly as he glanced at Richard in the rearview mirror. He turned the engine over and pulled out of the line and began advancing past the parked Cruisers and the incurious onlookers, none of whom seemed either surprised or embittered to see the *Mzungu* jumping the queue, as the Land

Rover straddled the verge of the narrow rutted road littered with trash and broken dreams.

But as they sped forward Richard's pulse flared, his heartbeat accelerating with anticipation. He felt as foolish and ashamed of his privilege as he was giddily hopeful of salvation. Which was, he realized, almost exactly the same way he had always felt when he was a teenager—and only a little hungover, and pleasurably muddled, after a bout of serious drinking and all-night sex with his girlfriend—while walking down the aisle towards the priest with his mom and dad on their way to receive the Eucharist on Sunday mornings.

But no one was obliging him to do this now. No one would be offended and hurt—no one would fail to understand him, and his many reasons for being incapable of believing in and embracing the rather childish fantasy of a miraculous communion with God—if he told Isamael that he had changed his mind, that it was too late now, that he had seen enough already and they should forget about Babu, and hurry to the clinic so that Richard could say hello to Dr. Bukuku and get back to camp before it got dark and they were prevented from traveling through the Serengeti Park.

No one but Isamael knew, in fact, that Richard was even here. And on his way to drink a brew of poison tree root that just might kill his cancer and prolong his life.

←⊹⊹ ←⊹⊹ ←⊹ ←

The lion was pressed tight and crouching—almost as if it were trying to couple with the bull—in the trampled grass, hunching fiercely over the right flank of the huge black buffalo, affixed once again to its hide, which was streaked now with bleeding cuts. Meanwhile the old bull sat wearily on its haunches, almost as if it had already given up.

Staring straight ahead, with no expression that Sofie could read in its big round eyes, the bull seemed almost contemplative. At one point it turned its head slowly, and sadly it seemed, towards the Land Rover, and looked directly at Sofie, revealing the bloody gash on the other side of its head where part of its mouth had been torn away with a bite or a swipe of the lion's paw.

Immediately Sofie wanted to avert her eyes, the same way she instinctively averted her eyes at the traffic lights when the homeless men in dirty overcoats approached her car, shaking their styrofoam cups of nickels and dimes. But instead she forced herself to stare back at the bull, without knowing what to think or do.

"Does he know he's doomed?" she whispered.

"The lion can only win," said Mwenge, his voice modulated with respect for the struggle they were witnessing, "by suffocating the bull. If the rest of the pride were around they would help this lion, by overwhelming the buffalo and forcing it onto its side. Then one of them could go for its throat."

Both animals continued to sit there, unmoving, for what seemed like such a very long time. They were locked together now in a contest that could mean the end of one of their lives, but neither of them seemed to be in any hurry—or even the least bit anxious, really—to make the next move, and perhaps seal its fate.

Or perhaps the old bull's apparently calm, almost unconcerned, and possibly resigned, manner was instead an indication of some profound and earthy intelligence at work, combined with its stubborn will to survive. Maybe the huge black bull was just gathering its strength, so that it might have a chance after all.

$$\rightarrow \rightarrow \rightarrow \rightarrow$$

As they neared the end of the long line of vehicles Richard saw a man in the distance—beyond the first of the many Land Cruisers— with a gray sprinkling of hair on his head and a very round face, an aged but obviously vibrant and still strong man, with thick meaty forearms, wearing a plaid shirt with the sleeves rolled up past his elbows, standing on short bowed legs over a thin woman who was holding a boy who lay squirming on his back upon her lap, a child who might not have been any older than six or seven. With the windows of the Land Rover rolled down Richard could hear the boy moaning through clenched teeth as the woman who must have been his mother tried to keep him still and at the same time pry his mouth open so that Mwasapile, who was surrounded by other people anxiously helping to restrain the boy, could pour the liquid in a tin cup that he held in his hand down the boy's throat.

Then the bull leaned forward—in an effort to get up—and simultaneously pushed with its hind legs, jumping to its feet and causing the lion to lift off the ground with the bull's momentum and leap neatly onto its back.

Now the lion rode the bull like a cowboy at a rodeo, around and around again, as the bull bucked and spun and dipped its head. And just like a cowboy, the lion eventually lost its grip just as soon as it tried to reaffirm it. Frantically biting and clawing again where it could, the rapid spinning of the bull bumped the lion forward and brought its chest within range of the bull's head. And as soon as this happened the bull expertly butted the lion into the air, and with a second slicing thrust caught the lion with a horn in the shoulder as the lion came down.

Almost instantly the lion was flung off the horns—its arms and legs akimbo—with such ease that it was hard for Sofie to believe that she was seeing this. And just as soon as the lion hit the ground it rolled, and tried to scramble to its feet, as the bull charged and plowed into it, raising a pall of dust and sending the lion tumbling through the grass.

But the lion was quick enough to dodge the next charge

and—lunging from underneath the bull—wrap its sinuous arms around the bull's neck almost as if it were hugging the huge black animal, while at the same time clamping its jaws over the bull's nose.

The buffalo groaned and complained, it braced its forefeet again and tried to pull and shake away from the lion. But the lion's claws and fangs were embedded deep in the bull's flesh, making separation impossible. Both animals were matted with bits of bloodied straw and dust, and the once glorious mane of the lion was now muddied with gore.

As the bull stood there with its bleeding nose trapped in the jaws of the lion—breathing only because the lion had failed to cover the bull's mouth as well—it seemed to Sofie that the fight had suddenly ended.

⇢ ⇥ ⇥ ⇥

"Turn around," said Richard.

"Nini?" said Isamael. "Ulisema nini?"

"I've seen enough! Let's get out of here!"

⇤ ⇤ ⇤ ⇠

Sofie was so focused on the lion and this particular bull that she hadn't noticed the other buffaloes that were edging forward, as a group, closer and closer, until Mwenge pointed them out to her. Slowly, tentatively, cautiously, they came, with heads lowered, emitting a collective grumbling that the lion must have heard.

But the lion's concentration was fixed entirely upon the animal it had in its grasp, and could not yet bring down alone. Nothing else seemed to exist—or matter—for the lion then, save that it not let go. It's pale yellow eyes were wide open, its dark pupils staring past the bull's head at the blue sky. And just as Sofie had wondered earlier what the old bull might have been thinking, now she wondered what thoughts, if any, were going through the lion's head.

⇢ ⇢ ⇢ ⇢

"We are already here!" exclaimed Isamael. "That is Babu, right there! And you have paid to see him when he finishes with this boy."

"I don't want to see him," shouted Richard. "I've changed my mind. I've seen enough already. Turn around!"

Isamael muttered something in Swahili, either a curse or an expression of his disbelief. But Richard didn't care. Though he was immediately sorry to have lost his temper with this young driver, nothing mattered to him now but getting out of there and as far away from all this nonsense as possible.

⇠ ⇠ ⇠ ⇠

Then there was a new sound, a desperate garbled grunting, and Sofie saw the blood bubbling out of the lion's mouth, as the captured bull tried to pull away while it snorted in reply to the grumbling of the rest of the herd, which was only a few meters away.

Either oblivious or unconcerned with the approach of the other buffaloes the lion simply held on. It seemed to be engrossed only with this one particular bull, and ignorant or uncaring of the risk it was taking by insisting on bringing this one bull down. It's stubborn refusal to let go was shocking, especially once the largest buffalo in the herd—the one with the thickest set of horns, fused solidly to the bone shield across its forehead known as a *boss*—detached itself from the herd and feinted a charge.

But it was as if the lion didn't even notice this. Until the big bull regathered its courage and lowered its head and shot forward on surprisingly nimble legs, taking a swipe at the lion with its scimitar-like horns.

It missed the lion, but the bull that was caught in the lion's jaws stumbled as a result of the staggering impact and fell onto its side this time. With an astounding alacrity the lion's whole body rearranged itself so that it's jaws could snap upon the wounded bull's throat.

The shrill distressful bellowing of the downed bull—whose helpless legs were sticking out, stiff and useless as if it had already been killed—was answered by deep nervous collective grunting, before another huge buffalo charged and caught the lion at its hip, slicing through the lion's flesh like a razor.

The lion growled in pain and fear, releasing the bull just as the first and bravest of the old buffaloes charged again and butted the lion head over heels. The lion rolled through the grass, its flailing arms and legs slapping the ground. As it tried to get to its feet the gouging in its side was momentarily visible, revealing the bright red muscle of its thigh.

But the lion had no chance to take any notice of the terrible wound because the old bull it had originally attacked was now coming at it, viciously swinging its horns and trying to clip the lion which rolled onto its back and swatted at the bulls face with its huge bloodied paws.

Isamael drove speedily now, back along the rough dirt road by which they had come, the wheels of the Land Rover spraying with debris the line of waiting vehicles and the crowd of people milling among them.

Richard wanted to command Isamael to slow down, he wanted to assert his authority and embrace his privilege now by insisting that it wasn't necessary to go so fast. But when a rock someone had thrown in anger flew through the open window and grazed the side of Richard's forehead he was suddenly overwhelmed with panic, and the fear of an African riot.

For a moment there was a standoff, with the bull's head lowered and ready to drive into the lion again, while the snarling and battered lion lay in a defensive position in the bloodied grass, its ears flattened against its skull, occasionally turning its head briefly towards the gaping wound below its hip, where the exposed muscle seemed to pulse.

The buffalo was dripping blood as well, from its mangled nose and mouth and all the other places where the lion had bit and clawed it as it tried to bring it down. But the old bull was still able to stand, even if a little unsteadily, and with its presence—and that of the rest of the herd behind it—pin the wounded cat to the ground.

"The lion is lost," said Mwenge. "Even if the buffalo do not kill it, the infection will."

As they sped down the hill towards Loliondo Richard touched his brow and felt the smear of blood. He assumed it was a superficial wound, though it was bleeding heavily enough to justify pulling his handkerchief out of the pocket of his pants and pressing it to his head.

While the lion lay there the herd of buffaloes inched forward, heads lowered, nostrils flaring, almost amoeba-like in their shifting and dubious unity. Though the lion no longer represented much of a threat to the buffaloes they treated it fearfully, and angrily as well, as they eventually split and moved out from behind the wounded bull and cautiously, tentatively, and always uncertainly, began to surround the big cat.

"Now they will finish him off," whispered Mwenge.

"Can we go?" pleaded Sofie.

Mwenge turned to look at her just as the chorus of grunting intensified. Both of them heard the lion's cry as the group of old bulls successively charged, one after the other. Now all Sofie could see was the excited and juddering swarming of the buffaloes and the clouds of dust they were kicking up. Every head was lowered and directed towards some point among them where the lion must lay, receiving one blow after another until it was finally hooked again and tossed in the air—hurled limply over the bulls' backs—causing the whole herd of buffaloes to turn together and rush to the place on the ground where the doomed lion had fallen.

"Please," screamed Sofie. "I've seen enough!"

By the time they got to the clinic Richard was aware of the throbbing in his lower back. Isamael had driven so fast over the ungraded roads that Richard had been bouncing in his seat. But he dared not say anything, he dared not complain.

But neither did he have any desire to see Dr. Bukuku, and subject himself to any opinions or judgments this man might make. Richard was afraid that Isamael would tell Dr. Bukuku what had happened before Richard had a chance to say anything and explain himself. Isamael might even tell the story while Richard stood there—right in front of the doctor—with a streaming cut over his left eye and a stupid uncomprehending expression on his face, while Isamael related his version of events in Swahili so that Richard wouldn't even be able to know how he was explaining Richard's change of mind to the doctor. And this—on top of everything that had already happened—would be an intolerable humiliation.

Risking Isamael's ire Richard told him to keep driving. "It's too late to stop here now," he said. "We need to get back to camp so that you can turn around and return to Loliondo before dark."

Isamael didn't say a word. Or even glance once in the rearview mirror. He didn't give any indication at all that he had heard what Richard had just said. Instead he kept his eyes on the road, both hands gripping the steering wheel, and continued speeding down the unpaved road.

Sofie sobbed freely now, without making any noise, as wave after wave of bottled up grief washed over her. She couldn't help it. She couldn't prevent herself from giving in at last to her deep remorse, but neither did she want to prevent this. She was ashamed to be indulging this emotion in front of—or directly behind—Mwenge. She didn't want to make him feel ill at ease. But she didn't want to miss the opportunity either to release at last at least some of her pent-up anger and frustration. So she sobbed, silently and uncontrollably.

Sofie's reaction baffled Mwenge. He kept looking at her in the rearview mirror, at the reddened eyes and the swollen lips that he had originally thought so pretty and fine, and exotic for being so thin and colorless that only lipstick could make them red. Sofie was staring out the side window as the tears streaked down her cheeks, seemingly indifferent to the wind raking the strands of blonde hair across her face. But she wasn't making any sound.

That was not the way the women Mwenge knew expressed their pain. He could understand screaming and ululating, but not this display of restrained, almost stifled, yet intense emotion. It confused and bewildered him, as he drove swiftly away from the place where they had witnessed the brutal death of the lion.

Though he tried to come up with something to say—something about what the *Wazungu* called the circle of life—he could not think of anything to say to Sofie, because he wasn't sure exactly why she was crying. Mwenge had dealt with many white men and women during his career as a guide, and he had seen a great deal of behavior that he could not—at first anyway—quite understand. But he believed that despite the color of our skin we were all the same inside. That men and women everywhere wanted the same few things from life: the comforts of home, the blessing of children, and the ability to provide for them.

What they had just witnessed was violent, yes, and shocking for her perhaps, because she had never seen it before. But this is what happened out here all the time, every day and every night, whether you witnessed it or not. Always and forever. Ever since the beginning of time.

Many animals died as well in even worse ways, by being eaten alive, for example. And some were born only to be eaten! Did she know this? The hyenas were infamous for attending the birth of any calf or fawn or cub, or other helpless creature, and taking it as soon as it hit the ground, while the distressed mother was still too weak and disoriented to do anything about it. At least this lion died fighting.

Maisha hayaendi katika mduara, thought Mwenge. Life does not go in a circle. But it is a game of cards. *Lakini maisha ni karata.*

And sometimes the cards you are dealt are not good cards, that's all. Sometimes you can improve upon what have in your hand. But sometimes you have to cut your losses and give up and fold. And sometimes you get caught having bet it all—as this lion did—and losing everything you have. Including the only thing you truly own, which is your one life.

Richard wanted to ask Isamael to keep what had happened between them. He knew he could use the money he had given Isamael—the fact that Isamael had accepted not a gratuity but a bribe; money though freely offered nonetheless offered to convince Isamael to do something that he hadn't been authorized to do—to blackmail the young driver. But Richard didn't want to do that.

On the other hand his first impression of Isamael—that he was morose—was being confirmed, and there was no longer any good feeling between them. The long drive back to camp was not only physically uncomfortable, it was emotionally awkward as well. Though he had plenty of time to come up with something, there was nothing that Richard could think of, no means by which he could ask Isamael to treat the failed trip to Samunge as a joke, and a friendly secret between them.

As a result Richard's mood blackened. And when they got back to the camp he got out of the Land Rover without saying a word of thanks to Isamael, who didn't bother to turn off the engine and only barely replied to the members of the staff who had come out to see who it was, muttering something brief and cutting in Swahili that Richard could never in a lifetime hope to understand.

Sofie sat there thinking that the glass wall between her and Mwenge was so thick that she must have been a fool for ever having believed that it would be possible to communicate with someone like him (someone like Zuri). It had been vainglorious of her to study Swahili in the first place. She could say a few things, certainly, and answer questions phrased in a way she was familiar with. But other than that she didn't have a clue. And although her intentions might have been good, what good were good intentions when nothing ever worked out the way it should anyway?

She knew, of course, that it wasn't just the lion, though she couldn't quit imagining the poor animal lying out there, after the herd of buffaloes had satisfied their desire for revenge, mortally wounded and waiting only for the first of the meat eaters—whether predators or scavengers—to come and start tearing at its flesh. Even if the lion were dead by the time this happened, even if it couldn't feel the pain, the thought of its flesh being scraped and sucked

71

clean—*scraped and sucked clean* until nothing was left to indicate that it had even been there in the first place, nothing that could confirm that it had ever *existed*—chilled her, overwhelming her with the crushing guilt once again.

At least, she thought, bitterly, the lion's death would serve a purpose. That of feeding others, and prolonging their lives.

But the same thing couldn't be said for what she had done. And all the justifications in the world—all of Richard's eloquent reasoning, all his persuasive arguments, all his empty promises, and all of his bullshit excuses—could never change that fact.

Richard went straight back to the tent, ordering hot water for a shower along the way. He opened his toiletry bag and removed the bottles of both the Tramadol and Oxycodone. Furious with himself for having made a fool out of himself, for having been willing to believe in the impossible—if only for a moment—he decided to take one of each. The two pain relievers should probably not be mixed—surely the doctors at the Mayo Clinic had warned him not to do this?—but one of each wasn't enough to cause him any more trouble, and certainly no more pain than that with which he was already dealing now.

Richard washed the pills down with bottled water and put the Tramadol and Oxycodone back in his bag. Then he paced about the tent, until he heard the man outside call that the hot water for the shower had been poured and hoisted.

Taking off his clothes Richard felt once again that desire to reach deep inside his own body and rip out the tumor. It was so small he could probably pinch it between two fingers, and if he could do that he could pop it like a zit. But he couldn't do that. And small as the tumor was, it was likely to kill him.

Before stepping onto the smooth crate-like wooden floor that was laid over the hole in the ground where the water drained harmlessly away somehow—everything about these camps was designed to make as little an environmental impact as possible—Richard stood in front of the mirror. He was still trim, and fit for fifty-three. Unlike so many of his colleagues his neck and shoulders hadn't thickened in that sickening way, as if bloated with toxins. His face was lean, and lined, but only enough, according to Sofie, to make him look distinguished, and even wise. And his hair had only recently begun to gray, adding to this effect.

Many people Richard met assumed he was somewhere in his mid-forties. No one would look at him now—in the warm orange glow inside the *nyumba* produced by the setting sun—and imagine that he was rotting from within.

Sofie wanted to apologize to Mwenge for having displayed so much private emotion in front of him. But she was too embarrassed to do anything but thank him for having taken her in search of the lion. As he held the door open for her and she climbed out of the Land Rover there was an awkward moment when he too seemed to want to say something other than, "Karibu sana." But instead he offered her only a slightly circumspect, yet gracious and dignified, nod of his head. And then that moment had passed, and she was walking away from him.

As Sofie approached the tent the sun slipped behind a low band of clouds moving in from the west, infusing these clouds with a violet hue and firing the breach between the hills below and the belly of these clouds with a radiant pink. The foreground of thorn-tree savanna continued dissolving into shadow, as the cover of night quickly spread. Sofie hesitated, before entering the tent, to watch the sun boldly reappear beneath the band of clouds and blaze one last time, cresting the hills with a flaming crown of light, before finally dropping behind them.

In many ways it was this that they had come so far for, the rare opportunity to share some of the ethereal—yet mundane, and evanescent—beauty in the world. Never before had she and Richard been allowed to live together, if only for a limited number of days. Never before had they been given the opportunity to spend such a seamless amount of time together during which time they might not only become impatient and testy with each other, like any married couple, but would also be able to share having seen and done so many extraordinary things. Things neither of them were ever likely to forget.

But Sofie was acutely aware—as the darkness all around the tent spread like spilled tar—of the transience of an experience that she had hoped might somehow be preserved, even once they had returned to the routine of their separated lives in the States. And as she turned her back on what little remained of the sunset and ducked into the tent she knew that nothing of this would really last. That this trip to East Africa would eventually become just one more memory. The sort of thing one could—actually—always forget.

III

When Richard came out of the shower with the towel wrapped around his waist Sofie was standing in the middle of the tent, looking at him with an indecipherable expression on her face. She wasn't exactly surprised to see him up and about, but neither did she demonstrate any joy or satisfaction at seeing him fresh out of the shower.

"Are you feeling better?" she said, automatically, and out of politeness, but dully, and not as if she really wanted to know. But then, noticing the cut above Richard's eye, she instinctively took a step towards him and raised a hand to gently touch the side of his face. "What happened to you?"

"Oh that," he said, recoiling as if her sudden tenderness might do him more harm than good. "It's just a scratch. I fell. I mean, I cut it on the nightstand. As I bent over to untie my laces."

Sofie considered the bedside table. Enmeshed in a net of lies that formed from the very beginning the fabric of their relationship, they had sworn to be honest with one another. Small lies, they had agreed, could be as damaging and destructive as large lies. But she knew that she hadn't held up her end of the bargain any better than he had.

"Here," she said, pushing past him and into the bathroom area of the tent, with its pump-flush toilet cubicle and cubby-holed shower stall, and mirror—in the narrow corridor between the toilet and shower—hanging over the sink. Using the non-potable water from one of the pitchers Sofie washed and rinsed her hands. Avoiding the temptation to look in the mirror—and see the same face that Richard could see—she found the Betadine in their first aid kit, and returned to the other room.

"You need to put something on that," she said. "Just in case."

Richard sat dutifully on the edge of the bed and patiently allowed her to apply the antiseptic solution with a Q-tip to the cut above his eye, thinking how pointless it was to worry about a little scratch when the cancerous cells strangling his pancreas were so busy multiplying. But Sofie's proximity to him—standing so close to him that Richard could have leaned forward and buried his face between her breasts, so close that he could smell, beneath the faint and slightly gamey odor of sweat and dust, the familiar and always welcome fragrance of her flesh—was a genuine comfort.

When he reached his arms around her waist though, she pulled away from him, saying, "That should do it."

→ →→ →→ →→

Mwenge made an excuse not to join them at their table that both Sofie and Richard accepted without protestation. There were no other guests in the camp that night, whereas previously—in Tarangire, for example—there had always been someone else, small groups of couples or heads of families with whom Richard and Sofie had sometimes shared a little small talk while having a drink and waiting for the call to wash their hands for dinner.

Left alone, at a table illuminated by the light of only one of the two hurricane lamps that hung from the central pole of the dining tent, they had nothing to say to each other at first. Or perhaps too much to say to each other. So much that neither of them knew how to begin.

Richard felt better already, with the delayed action Tramadol finally kicking in. Perhaps he should pop a pair of those pills more often, and just ride this thing out on a wave of narcotically induced bliss. Or often enough, anyway, to allow him to get through the rest of the safari without further incident.

The wine too—which he probably ought not to be drinking, at least according to the fastidious advice of the overly conservative doctors back home, whose primary concern was avoiding being sued—was helping to soften and quiet his mood. He was beginning to regard the trip to Samunge as the joke he wanted it to be, and as he refilled Sofie's glass with wine he felt the irrepressible urge to share this joke with her.

But he didn't know how to phrase it, he was at a loss for the right words. He didn't feel—sitting at that small cloth-draped table on the edge of the Serengeti—that he would be able to access and draw upon the charm necessary to turn the pursuit of a miracle into a joke.

And reinforcing this unusual lack of confidence was a much deeper sentiment, which confused him at first. Until he realized that what he needed most at this moment of his life—a life that was possibly nearing its end—was to rise out of the ashes. At least spiritually. Something he wasn't very likely going to be able to do.

"Did you find your lion?" he said, taking a sip of his wine, which seemed to instantly sour on his tongue. Richard picked up the bottle and studied the label, but without the reading glasses he refused to wear in public he couldn't distinguish the small letters in the weak light of the hurricane lamp. And he wasn't about to ask Sofie to read the label for him. Instead he'd just have to trust that what he was drinking was the very thing he had asked for.

When Sofie didn't respond Richard set the bottle down and saw that she wasn't even looking at him. Instead her head was turned so that she was facing the bonfire that simmered—no flames, just the subdued embers burning bright and hot but low—at the periphery of the permanent camp site.

The light of the single hurricane lamp created a brassy golden glow, and in that mellowed illumination the silhouette of Sofie's head seemed almost iconic. Richard could have been looking at a sepia portrait of a woman whose slightly parted lips suggested the grief that everyone knows, sooner or later.

Simultaneously Richard felt the extreme tenderness of having always truly cared for her, independent of anything he had ever greedily wanted from her for himself, including the warmth of her body pressed tight against his. That, and the cold and seemingly unsurpassable distance that separated them at that moment, her remoteness.

Raising the glass of wine to his lips, and feeling tipsier than usual, as a consequence perhaps of mixing the alcohol with the Tramadol, he repeated his question.

"Yes," she said, at last. "We did find the lion."

Sofie wasn't sure when the point of no return had been reached. She didn't even know if it was possible to ever figure something like that out. But she knew that they were beyond that point now, out *there* somewhere, without even so much as a compass to guide them.

"He was striking," she said, picking up the glass of wine that Richard had topped up for her. "A young male. With hardly any mane. Recently forced to live on his own. Just like Mwenge had said. A young lion that had wandered into an older lion's territory."

"I think Mwenge takes some liberties with his imagination," said Richard. "How could he know—how could you tell by just looking at this lion—that he had wandered into another's territory?"

"He was so thin, Richard. So lean and thin. He was obviously very hungry. Starving. He was bold, yes. But he had so little confidence, really, even though he tried to cover it up with his boldness. And that made me pity him even more. As soon as I saw him I knew he was lost. And that made me feel terribly sorry for him. If it wouldn't have been for that, I don't think anything would've happened."

"What do you mean, nothing would have happened? What happened? What did you see?"

"An animal that saw its chance and took it," she said, sitting a little straighter in her chair. "Just another animal, like us, as eager to survive and get along and have what everyone else has as any other animal."

Richard sighed, audibly. It was a habit that had always annoyed her. But there is always so much in a new lover that is overlooked, in order to allow the loving to take place.

Sofie wanted to tell him now, she didn't want another night to end with Richard not knowing. It had all been a mistake, the kind of thing that just happens. Sofie had meant only to give Zuri the money he needed, enough to fill up a jerry can so that he wouldn't lose his job. But when she offered him the *shilingi* notes he wrapped his warm dark hand around her fingers. And when he pulled her towards him she didn't resist.

"Maybe we should go sit at the fire," she suggested.

⇢ ⇢ ⇢ ⇢

Once again a member of the staff was summoned. After rearranging the logs in the bonfire and adding some branches the man squatted on his haunches and started blowing on the embers. Soon the brightening flames lit his face.

"Asante sana," said Sofie.

"Karibu sana," said the man, as he got to his feet and turned to saunter back to the tents.

For a while the two of them sat there, side by side, close enough to have held each other's hand, without either of them making a move to do so.

The night beyond the circumference of the firelight was pitch black, and teeming with wildlife. It was something Richard could feel, something anyone who came here could always feel. The endless struggle going on out there, for lack of a better word.

The struggle to survive, of course, if only another night, like that lion Sofie had seen. The struggle to stay alive and endure, by either eating enough, or avoiding being eaten. Even, he supposed, the struggle to reproduce. Though the rhythms of mating—unlike those of hunting—were not necessarily dictated by whether or not the desired object could be seen.

"There's something I need to tell you," said Sofie, startling Richard out of the slightly melancholic ruminations that he was beginning to indulge in. Because it was the memory of her that his thoughts had veered towards, and the way their own love making had been dictated not by the season or time of day, nor even by the moon, but only ever by sheer opportunity, and the simple fact that they had both wanted each other so very much. Richard was wondering, when Sofie interrupted his thoughts, about the priorities, on the long list of all the many things that a dying man would regret never being able to do again.

"I don't like the sound of that," he said, sitting forward in the camp chair and bending down to splash a little more Glenfiddich into his tumbler.

As he sat back in the chair he felt Sofie's hand on his forearm.

"We agreed not to tell any lies," she said.

"That's what all lovers do. It's practically a reflex. After making love for the first time."

"We agreed that small lies were as dangerous as big lies."

"That's because the only way that *we* could be, you and I, *us*," he said, using her terminology, and finally turning to face her, "was via a patchwork of those petty lies. You and I wove a massive web out of them, at the center of which was the one great compound lie, that of my infidelity. And the corresponding unlikelihood of anyone's felicity."

Sofie withdrew her hand. One moment it had been there, resting lightly on Richard's wrist, and now it was gone. He knew better than to concede the stage he now stood on to any bitterness, but the whisky wanted to talk. Richard wanted with all his heart for her to know, he wanted to scream out that there would be no more arguments over how they might manage to see each other during the Christmas holidays, no more tears at her so often being left alone on every sentimental anniversary when he was surrounded by the family he loved and felt shackled to, because he wouldn't be there anymore. And yet, more than anything else, he didn't want to pity himself.

"Whether or not you want to hear it," she said, "I'm going to tell you. You can walk away if you like. But I'm going to say everything I need to say."

"Look out there," said Richard, motioning towards the darkness with his tumbler. "There is more going on out there than we could ever imagine. But we can't see it. Can you imagine how absurd it would be to illuminate the entire Serengeti with floodlights in order to betray all those secrets?"

"Are you drunk?" she said.

"I'm working on it," he admitted.

For a while neither of them spoke. There was only the crackling of the fire at their feet, and beyond that the unintelligible babble of the African night.

"I'm sorry," he said, and he meant it, once again. He finished what was left in his glass and bent down to refill it, but Sofie caught his arm. Richard sat back in his seat, feeling very tired now.

"What I meant to say," he said, "is that you don't have to tell me anything. Nothing at all."

"But I want to tell you, Richard. Don't you see?"

"No, I don't," he said. "I can't see anything anymore. Not a damn thing."

He wasn't making it any easier, but this time she took his resistance—
and the risk that he might blow up with her—as a challenge, one
that she wasn't going to back down from. Hadn't the Cape buffalo
refused to back down? But on the other hand, so had the lion.

"Richard," she said, in a voice she knew he would recognize as
conciliatory and perhaps even mildly solicitous, "I just want to be
honest with you. I just want to be honest with myself. We've come
all this way—"

"On the only real trip we'll have ever made together."

"What do you mean?"

But it was the resentment in what he had just said, more than
the words themselves—since Richard wasn't given to hyperbolic
statements, not even when loaded—that most alarmed her.

"I know," he said, "that you think that all I did at college was
party and try to figure out how to make as much money as possible
once I got out of school and paid off my student loans. But I did do
some serious reading while I was there."

"What are you trying to say?"

"I made a big mistake when I was young, Sofie. Despite
my hedonistic streak I was afraid of being frivolous. I thought
happiness—what people understood to count for happiness—was
something minted in Disneyland. I took myself far too seriously,
even though I was committed to pleasure."

"I don't understand," she moaned. "Are you feeling ill again?"

"I'm feeling fine," said Richard. He lifted the empty tumbler to
his lips and when he realized it was empty he bent down again to
pour some more. Sofie tried to stop him again, but he shook off her
hand and grabbed the bottle. He set the tumbler between his thighs
and for a moment she was afraid he was going to drink straight out
of the bottle. Instead he sloshed so much into the glass that he wet
himself with the whisky and muttered, "Damn."

Very gently Sofie took the bottle from him. Richard turned his head enough to look at her. In the firelight she could see an expression on his face she'd never seen before. It was as if the years of experience that separated them—something neither of them had ever thought too much about, not, anyway, as any sort of impediment—finally manifested themselves. It was as if the lines in Richard's face, accentuated by the shifting light of the flames, were engraved in stone.

"There's nothing but pleasure and pain, Sofie. Nothing at all. And no need to fear death. That's what Epicurus said."

"What?"

"He said something else as well. That we should live life secretly. Intimately. With no regrets. That's all I meant to say."

> ⇢ ⇢ ⇒ ⇒⟩

Having made this enigmatic pronouncement Richard felt like standing up, so that he might lend finality to what he'd just said. But he wasn't sure he could manage it, and successfully climb to his feet. So he just sat there, staring into the black night beyond the glow of the bonfire.

"Maybe we should go to bed," suggested Sofie.

Her voice was as soft and inviting as it had ever been. Richard closed his eyes hard against the sudden upsurge of emotion. He remained determined not to pity himself. That was the one betrayal he would not indulge in. Hadn't he led an eventful, a full and rich life? Didn't he have a devoted wife—and long-time companion as well—waiting for him with his son and daughter, back home in the States? Wasn't that enough to look forward to? And didn't he have this woman beside him right now, who had reawakened him when he had come to accept the sexless daily grind as a mode of being? Reawakened him to the joy of falling in love! How could anyone fail to appreciate all of that?

"What's the matter, Richard? What's wrong?" she said.

Now Sofie's hand sought Richard's fingers. The tumbler of whisky was still wedged between his thighs, which were wet with the spill. He felt like surrendering, and just giving up. For a moment he wished he was a child again, small enough to be carried home and put to bed. But instead he was a middle-aged man with a festering tumor the size of a marble that was intent upon destroying everything.

"I'm not going to make it, Sofie."

Stranger than what he'd just admitted was the way both of them were using the other's name, as if to emphasize the fact that it was to him or her—and only to him or her—that they were speaking.

Sitting close to the seductive heat of the fire, with no other ground light but that produced by the lantern hanging at the entrance to the dining tent behind them, with the cold bright glaze of stars suspended high above them, Sofie felt as if she'd finally achieved the degree of intimacy with Richard that falling in love with him had made her always want so much. She realized that whatever he was talking about, she was the only one who was hearing what he said. And the only one who could do anything about it. It was as if, for a moment, Andrea and the twins no longer existed.

"Let me take you back to the tent," she pleaded. "You must be exhausted."

"I am exhausted. That's the thing. But it's not the only thing."

Sofie waited, uncertain how to respond to this. Richard could become lively under the influence of alcohol, and nasty too, sometimes. But it wasn't like him to become so mawkish, and discouraged.

She stood up and put her hands on her hips, before turning towards the dining tent. The guard was sitting on one of the folding chairs with the assault rifle cradled in his arms, though it occurred to Sofie that he might have been dozing.

"I'll be right back," she said. Touching Richard lightly on the shoulder she walked away from him and towards the man whose job it was to watch over them.

As soon as she had left him alone Richard pushed himself to his feet, spilling the tumbler filled with whisky down one leg of his pants and nearly tipping the chair over. He was rarely ever sloppy drunk, and even now he doubted that he was really as drunk as all of that. In fact he felt—despite the dizzying throb of the blood pulsing in his veins, and the corresponding laboring of his fifty-three-year-old heart—a peculiar clarity, what felt like an almost clairvoyant ability to see.

But he needed to piss. Real bad. So he pulled the little LED flashlight out of one of the many pockets of the safari jacket that Sofie had surreptitiously shopped for and found and purchased for him, and he strapped it over his head.

With only a few stumbling steps he was deep in the bush. It sounded like he was walking on paper, the grass beneath his feet was so dry and friable, so crunchingly resonant and loud. Richard plodded forward, the cold blue light attached to his head shakily stabbing the darkness that wrapped itself around him just as soon as he had abandoned the circle of light created by the bonfire.

He hadn't walked for long before a pant leg caught on one of the low thorny bushes that he had reminded himself to be careful of. With a grunt he bent over, and eventually worked the lightweight cotton of his trousers free of the hook of the thorn.

When he stood up again he saw a pair of bright yellow eyes, shining in the light of his headlamp.

→ ·→ ·→ ··→

The guard had, in fact, fallen asleep. Sofie couldn't blame him, and was loathe to wake him. It must be a dull thankless job. She peered into the gloom of the dining tent, where the light had been blown out, but saw no other staff members hanging around, like they sometimes did. They must have already cleaned up, though there should have been someone whose duty it was to remain on hand and look after the guests. To provide them with more drink, if they wanted it. Though perhaps once they had handed over the bottle of Glenfiddich the members of the staff had assumed that their services would no longer be needed that night.

Rather than disturb the guard, Sofie pulled the mosquito flap aside and stooped into the dining tent. She felt her way among the tables and chairs towards the back of the tent, which had a rear entrance for the staff. She knew that the kitchen was back there, somewhere behind the dining tent, and that the staff bunked in tents near the kitchen. As she slipped through a second mosquito flap she could hear the voices of men speaking softly, yet uninhibitedly. They might have been playing cards, their quiet laughter was so musical in the dark.

Sofie hesitated, recalling the sensation of being drawn against Zuri's naked and hairless chest. She was wearing nothing but her bikini, with the pareo wrapped around her waist. He still held onto her fist, which was closed around the *shilingi* notes she held in her hand. The movement he had made to draw her to him was so fluid and unexpected that she hadn't had time to react. She just followed his lead, like a thoroughly domesticated animal being led on a rope. And in the same way she allowed him to reach his other hand around her waist, and draw her hips firmly against his own.

Richard remembered what Mwenge had said about the eyes of nocturnal animals, that they have a topetum membrane that reflects the ambient light. Mwenge said that the night gaze of most animals is actually red, like a coal-red beacon. But what Richard saw was a bright piercing yellow. Two pin-points of luminous, and almost jeweled, yellow in the dark.

The distance between Richard and whatever it was that was staring at him could not be judged. Separating them was a space so black it seemed liquid, like the boiling asphalt in the large portable vats used to patch up roads in the summer. Richard understood as well that it was only due to the flashlight he was wearing on his head that he had any idea where the other animal was. Without the flashlight he would be blind. Whereas this animal would still be able to see him.

He knew though—or at least he felt certain—that it wasn't a lion, or any other large predator. The eyes were too close together, suggesting the head was much smaller than that. And although he couldn't be certain how tall the animal was, the pair of shining eyes didn't appear to be much higher off what Richard estimated to be the ground than his knees.

No matter what it was, neither Richard nor the animal with the yellow eyes moved. But it wasn't long until another pair of eyes trotted within range of the beam of his flashlight and turned to stare at him, the way all animals looked at you in the bush, unabashedly, and with keen interest. And then, a moment later, a third pair of eyes appeared.

⇢ ⇢ ⇢ ⇢

On Richard's recommendation Sofie had gone to see this man, Dr. Weber. But it hadn't worked out. From the beginning she'd felt as though she couldn't entirely trust him, something they actually talked about. He assured her that although he and Richard had become somewhat friendly, he was sitting before her as a professional therapist, and he wouldn't have agreed to see her if he didn't believe that he could help her work her way through whatever it was that was bothering her. He agreed, though, that the chemistry between a therapist and a patient was essential to successful treatment. And he told her that he understood when she informed him that she had decided not to come back.

Before that though he had insisted that the lies we tell to others are nothing compared to those we tell ourselves. He said that sometimes an untruth was justified, as in cases in which the cold hard facts might be more than someone else could handle at that moment. It wasn't easy to judge the needs of this other person though, and separate them from our own ingrained inclination to protect ourselves and fend off all challenges to the pride and insecurity of our ego.

"But as long as you're honest with yourself," he'd said, "you'll figure it out. Eventually."

Now there were five or six, possibly more, pairs of eyes out there. Richard felt an almost overwhelming impulse to turn his head and see how far he'd wandered from the protective perimeter of the bonfire's glow. But the only thing he was truly afraid of right now was losing sight of all those pairs of yellow eyes. And not knowing how close the hyenas were.

Mwenge had warned them not to leave their shoes outside the tents, saying these animals ate everything, including dirty socks. Behaviorally similar to canines—though they were more closely related to felines—they always hunted in packs. Contrary to popular belief, spotted hyenas killed almost everything they ate and lions were more likely to scavenge from them than the other way around. They were usually shy of humans, but always much bolder at night.

All of these facts passed through Richard's mind like shooting stars, while he stood there, looking at the immobile pairs of glinting eyes that nonetheless seemed to float in the dark. He had heard, of course, about the way hyenas tore their prey apart without bothering to kill their victims first, like lions usually did. Many animals were eaten out here while still alive. Still breathing, still feeling, still thinking. Protected only from the gruesome reality of their fate by the numbing and desensitizing effect of shock.

But what was the probability, he wondered, of a middle-aged man dying like that, within say, twenty or thirty meters of a permanent camp site? Surely it had to be even lower than that of his pulling through, and making it back in the States after all.

So Richard reached up and flicked off his head lamp, and made the hyenas disappear. Then he turned around and started walking back towards the light of the bonfire, the way a drowning man swims with all the strength he has left in his arms towards the distant shore.

ACKNOWLEDGMENTS:

This short novel resulted from a long process of distillation during which many people contributed to enhancing my ability to write it, if only by putting up with me and believing in me more than I did myself. I want to thank each and every one of them and especially mention the Primary Believers: Abelardo, Angel, Pam, Philip and Mark, both Kims, Rhonda, Bill and Christina, as well as the members of Hot Breakfast.

Anton Baer has been there for me throughout and kindly read and expertly critiqued the story. Kimberly Davis did an outstanding editorial and layout job, and Verónica Sosa generously provided her talents as well. Having said that I am the only one responsible for any errors or shortcomings in the book.

Finally I would like to thank Geofred Osoro for his patience in teaching me Swahili and ensuring that the Swahili text was correct. And both Casmir Shija and Frank Massawe for generously sharing their knowledge, understanding, humanity and spirit with me and my family.

CPSIA information can be obtained
at www.ICGtesting.com
Printed in the USA
LVOW03s1905181017
552932LV00002B/4/P